The Shrouded Sea

Leon Dedeaux

DEDICATION

For my wife and daughter, my inspiration and love.

With Thanks to

Hailey Renner, a truly excellent editor

Map of the Six Nations and the Shrouded Sea

Chapter 1

Alaric rushed through the streets of Port Theron, racing to be the first to reach the counting house. The first got their choice of jobs, and if he got there early enough, he'd get more than his share. He needed all the work he could get. So did all the other messengers, but that wasn't his problem.

The eastern sky lightened to a pre-dawn gray, with a line of pale gold at the horizon. Darkness clung to the city like a hangover, but Alaric's feet knew every stone of the dim streets.

He shook off the lingering weariness of long hours and little sleep, letting the exertion bring his tired mind and senses to life. His feet slapped the ground lightly, and he was nowhere near winded. He heard the noises of a waking city, the quiet dissipating in fits and starts. A seagull cried. Another answered. Two street merchants argued over a good selling spot. The violent men who ruled the dark slipped into the shadows to sleep off the night's crimes—most of them, anyway. The air smelled as clean as it ever would, freshened by the night's light rain.

Alaric reached the counting house. He'd beaten the others, the punks and orphans and dock rats who scraped a living from the streets of Port Theron, the greatest commercial port in Thervingi.

Expendable human surplus. That's what they were called by the very people who relied on their cheap labor. Alaric had beaten the odds just by making it to seventeen. He'd beaten them doubly by making himself valuable. The moneymen knew he would get the messages through, no excuses. They knew his mind for numbers. They knew they could tell him something once, and he'd deliver it word for word.

He studied the counting house while he waited for it to open. Two heavy doors dominated the face of the building, eight feet wide and ten feet tall and guarded by watchmen on either side. They were intricately carved from dark Kartargan wood shipped five hundred miles from the south. Carriages could be pulled through those doors, horses and all, not that they ever did. The frame around the door gleamed with fine quartz from northern Solok, carved by artisans from all of the Six Nations. The message was unmistakable: Here stands the wealth of the world.

Alaric glanced toward the horizon to check the time. The first rays of morning sparkled on the sea to the southeast. There would be just enough time to carry messages to the ship captains before they left with the changing tide.

He shifted from side to side, too anxious to enjoy the cool of the morning. It would be hot soon enough. Port Theron lay on the southern coast of Thervingi, and its stifling wet heat punished foreigners and oppressed the weak—just like everything else here.

Alaric carried that weight every day and hardly noticed it.

"Looks like you're the first one here again," Pacha said. The night watchman was tall for a Thervingi, close to six feet. He wore a helmet and breastplate and held a long poleaxe. He had brown-bronze skin, dark eyes, and straight black hair, like Alaric.

"I like to eat. I like to sleep indoors," Alaric said. "So I get up early and get the work."

"Fair enough."

His partner, Devi, was a bit shorter but thick as a stone wall. "You like the sunrise? I think it's going to be a good one. Lots of gold, maybe a bit of pink."

"Let's ask him," Pacha said to Devi. "Alaric's smart. He might know."

"Ask me what?"

"Do you think the plague will come down here?" Pacha asked. "Devi thinks it will stay in Hiberia, but I'm worried."

"It's too hot down here," Devi said. "Hiberia is dry and cold. The same things don't live both places."

Alaric frowned. "I hope you're right."

"But?" Devi asked.

"Sicknesses live in our bodies," Alaric said. "I don't think they care about the weather."

"Well, that's a cheerful thought," Devi said.

Pacha changed the subject. "Got any leads yet?"

Alaric shook his head.

"I'm really sorry to hear that," Pacha said. "If anyone around here could become a scholar, you could. You got more brains than most rich men. If I was rich, I'd pay your way."

"If I was rich, I'd do lots of things," Devi said. "But we don't get the gold. We just guard it."

"Maybe it's for the best," Pacha said. "It's a bad time to head north anyway. The whole Hiberi University is probably sick, unless they shut it down to stop the spread."

"Hey," Devi said, "it's time."

The doors slowly opened from inside. The moneymen kept guards on the front, back, and inside of the building, all day and night. The guards discouraged impulsive fools. Wise men knew better than to steal from the most powerful men in the city. Even a successful heist would be a death sentence. And speaking of power…

"Alaric! As I live and breathe! Here you are, awake before the sun and ready to work." The boss of the west wharfs smiled widely and gestured with his ring-covered hands.

"Hello, Mr. Gatta."

"While you work, consider my offer. You will make much better money running numbers for me than running errands for them."

"I'll think about it, Mr. Gatta."

"Think well. Port Theron is a dangerous city. You would be protected if you worked for me." The boss's smile did not quite reach his eyes. "Use that sharp mind of yours. Run the numbers in your head. You know I'm right."

"Thank you," Alaric said. "I'll think about it."

"Don't think too long." The boss turned to go. "You know I'll treat you better than Dughall or Jaheel. You're my own countryman. We Thervingi have to stick together."

Alaric nodded along with the lie. He and Mr. Gatta shared the same warm brown skin, straight black hair, and dark eyes, but that was all. Maybe Mr. Gatta had been a street rat like Alaric when he was young, but that was a long time ago. Years of rich food and fine wine had rounded the boss's face, and years of power and wealth had turned his desperate hunger into calculating cruelty.

As far as sticking together, Port Theron had plenty of Thervingi street rats and orphans. If Mr. Gatta wanted to show solidarity, he had no shortage of targets.

Not that the Vorali or Bosphori bosses would be any kinder. They might offer more pay, but in the end, it wouldn't be enough. None of it would. Alaric wouldn't get what he wanted, wouldn't be who he wanted to be, counting debts and payments for a wharf boss. He'd still be a rat, just a rat with strained eyes and nicer clothes.

"Think about it, boy," Gatta said.

"Yes, sir." Alaric headed into the counting house. If he wanted to eat today, he needed to get to work. Those messages wouldn't deliver themselves.

Even with Mr. Gatta's pay, he'd never have enough to attend a university. He'd be no closer to earning the one thing no one could buy or inherit: a degree, and the self-worth that came with it.

Nobles demanded respect by their birth. Rich men paid for deference. People envied them, but respect must be earned. A scholar's robes proved they'd done the work. Even the richest man couldn't buy a degree.

Alaric wanted that more than anything. Never again would he be orphan, street trash, dock rat. He'd be scholar, professor, doctor.

He knew he could do it. He just had to find a way in.

Alaric collected a stack of messages. He slipped them into his backpack, then latched it securely. The messages had to get through, or he didn't get paid. No excuses.

The clerks trusted him to get them through quickly, no matter what. He knew the ritzy prime docks as well as he knew the ramshackle common docks. Six Nations navy, royal yachts, trading company freighters, or smugglers, it didn't matter. Alaric delivered.

He thought about Mr. Gatta's offer while he walked. He could handle keeping the gambling house records, and the pay would be good. But Alaric knew the kinds of people Gatta dealt with. Gambling was the least of the old man's vices. Alaric wasn't that desperate. Yet. But every day he got closer to saying yes.

"Alaric!" A kid trembled against the alley wall. His wide eyes looked this way and that, wildly. Sweat stuck his dark hair to his face. "Alaric! Please!"

"I don't stick my neck out for anybody," Alaric muttered. He took a deep breath and knew it was a lie. "Lennick, what's wrong?"

"They're after me."

Alaric slipped into the alley and glanced over his shoulder. A big man and a shorter older man shoved their way through the crowd about a hundred yards off.

"Muscle and brains. What did you do? You've got two of Dughall's men after you." Alaric recognized their light hair and sunburned skin. Vorali, from the misty north. Port Theron's searing sun lay heaviest on them.

"I don't know," Lennick said. "I took a job from Lakshi—"

"You did what?" Alaric felt a weight in his belly. "He gave you a package? Something to deliver to his place up the hill?"

"Yes. How did you know?"

"Never take a job like that. No matter how good the pay is, never take a package from Lakshi. You'll end up dead." Alaric took another glance down the street. The two men were getting closer. "Whatever's in that box is expensive and illegal. You know that. And these two men want it."

"But the pay was so good," Lennick said, "and I was out of money."

"I've been there. I've been broke, and I've been hungry," Alaric said quietly. "But you never take a job like that. You know the old saying: 'You can't spend a copper farthing when you're dead, much less a king's ransom.'"

"But—"

"Why do you think he paid so well for a kid like you?"

Lennick hung his head. "It's too dangerous. Anybody older would have been too smart to take the job."

"Right." Alaric glanced around the corner. "They're getting close. We need to run for it. On three, two, one!"

Alaric took off running, dragging Lennick behind. The two men bulled their way into the alley. Their heavy footsteps pounded on the paving stones behind him.

"They're catching up!" Lennick said.

"Keep up!" Alaric pointed to another alley just ahead. When he reached it, he shoved Lennick through. "Keep moving. How are you so slow?"

"I'm trying! Please!" Lennick gasped the words out, struggling as he ran.

"There! Up those boxes to the roof." Alaric pointed to a row of boxes beneath a low window. "We'll lose them on the rooftops."

"What? I can't do that!" Lennick half gasped, half screamed the words.

Alaric glanced back. The two men grew closer every moment. Instinctively, his hand went to a pouch at his side and touched a paper packet there. One shot. Not yet.

"Can you fight them, Alaric?"

"I can take the little one. Can you handle the big guy?"

"No."

"Then follow me." Alaric ran past the piled crates, cursing the missed opportunity. He ducked through another alley and burst out into a public street. "Stay close. We'll lose them in the crowd." Alaric darted across the street into the most crowded area he could find.

"You think we lost them?" Lennick pressed against a storefront, gasping for breath. He kept as low as he could without sitting.

Alaric stood on his tiptoes, looking over the crowd. "They're still coming. I don't know if they'll attack in public, but we haven't lost them."

"Oh, I knew I should have left an offering at the temple of protection," Lennick said.

"If you could afford to pay off the priests, you wouldn't have taken this job," Alaric said. "Not like the Heavenly Court would bother with our kind."

"Hey!" Lennick said, "That's…um…."

"An ugly truth," Alaric said, "like most of our lives. Now be quiet."

"What do we do?"

"Be quiet! Let me think." Alaric glanced at the buildings around him. Suddenly, he smiled.

"No! You're thinking of leaving me alone with them," Lennick cried. "Please, don't leave me!"

"Look!" Alaric pointed at an alley. "We're almost there. Two streets over, one block up, and we're there. Drop off the package and stay put until the thugs go away. They won't try anything on Lakshi's turf. Not if they value their lives."

"All right." Lennick hands shook, but he was starting to catch his breath again. "I'm ready."

"Now." Alaric ran, leading Lennick through the alley. The two men shoved their way through the crowds toward them. Alaric burst out of the alley. He weaved between the people on the street and plunged into the next alleyway. Lennick was breathing hard but kept up.

Heavy footsteps grew nearer.

Lennick pointed ahead at a stack of crates blocking the exit to the alley. "We're trapped!"

"We can make it! Stick with me." Alaric ran to the nearest crate, thankful that some had fallen. He leapt to the top of the first one and pulled Lennick up behind him. "Keep moving." He climbed onto the second and pulled Lennick up.

Dughall's thugs were almost upon them. Alaric glanced at the two men. Their red faces twisted in anger. He shoved Lennick onto the next level of crates. "Go over the top. Drop down carefully. Don't stop running until you reach Lakshi's."

This time the kid didn't argue.

That left Alaric alone with two angry men. The small one outweighed him by at least thirty pounds. The big one was twice his size.

"The kid got away, but we're gonna take this out of your hide." The big man cracked his knuckles, stalking slowly forward. He moved with purpose, closing off angles, controlling his area and his movements. "Go ahead. Try to escape."

Alaric reached down into his pouch again. A single packet of paper held powdered red pepper and fireplace ashes. One shot. He waited, legs ready to launch, until the big man was almost on top of him.

His hand whipped out, flinging the paper packet into the big man's face. It burst into a gray cloud, filling the man's nose and eyes with burning, stinging powder. He roared and grabbed at his face. He staggered backward, knocking the smaller man aside.

The big man recovered in a moment, but that moment was all Alaric needed. He scrambled up the boxes and over the top, landed easily on the other side, and vanished into the crowd.

So much for not sticking my neck out for anyone, Alaric thought. He scowled for a moment, then grinned. The look on that dumb ox's face was worth all the effort. All right, get to work, he told himself. You've got bills to pay and more ground pepper to buy.

Alaric stood on the seawall, all messages from the counting house safely delivered. To his left were the prime docks where wealthy and powerful people anchored their ships. Most days he got here early and picked up five or six delivery jobs. The wealthy captains were happy to press a coin in his hand to send a message back up the hill. But helping Lennick had delayed him, and others had beaten him to the jobs. Today, they had nothing for him.

So, he looked to the common docks, where everyone else put in. The ships there were smaller and shabbier, and so were the captains. Most were independent merchants and cargo haulers just trying to make a living. A few big trading companies controlled most of the work. They devoured more and more each year, rotting out the small traders' livelihoods like wood worms.

Then there were the smugglers, moving boxes and crates that only looked legal. Their ships were nicer, and their eyes harder. Rumors said some were secretly pirates. Alaric had no business with them.

Alaric listened to the calls of the seagulls and the barking of the harbor seals. The smell of the sea mixed with the smell of smoke from a hundred coal fires. The sound of the waves vanished beneath the chatter of a thousand conversations and the noise of ten thousand footsteps.

A man, a woman, and a tall, stocky girl made their way down the prime docks. Alaric watched as ship after ship turned them away. At first, he watched them out of amusement. Sometimes it was fun watching someone else feel frustrated and helpless for once. But as they grew closer, he saw what they were wearing.

Hiberi scholar robes? Alaric stared for another moment to be sure. If these were Hiberi scholars, they could help him get into the Academy. If he helped them, perhaps his life could change. He let them walk past, then followed.

"Don't be discouraged, Lamarca," the man said. He looked a bit older than his colleague; there were streaks of silver at his temples.

"Maxime, we've talked to nobles and navy ships and corporate freighters," Lamarca said, "How many other vessels will have the capacity to take us to our destination?" She looked a fit and well-off forty, with warm red-brown skin and barely a hint of gray in her thick black hair.

The girl scoffed. "We knew they wouldn't help us, Professor Lamarca." She stood nearly six feet tall, with strong shoulders and long auburn hair. She looked to be Alaric's age and wore a loose, homespun dress.

"It was worth asking," Maxime said, "because of the resources they could bring to bear on our project. We aren't exactly following the common trade routes."

"Will anyone will take this risk?" Lamarca said. "It does seem like madness, even to me." She turned to the girl. "No offense, Zarah."

"Someone will," Zarah said. "My visions wouldn't have driven me here just to strand me. I may die doing this, but it won't be here."

Lamarca forced a smile. "I admire your optimism, Miss Remei."

"Come on," Alaric whispered from the shadows. "Say where you're going."

"I suppose if anyone will take us through the mists of the Shrouded Sea, we'll find them here." Maxime gestured to the common docks. "May the High King of Heaven have mercy on us."

Zarah gritted her teeth at the word mercy.

"Perhaps mercy would have been choosing an adult to carry this burden," Lamarca said.

"No pity for me, professor," Zarah said. "I'll see this through if it kills me. There's a plague spreading, and the cure is on that island."

"We'll find a ship." Maxime looked up and down the docks, then back at Professor Lamarca and Zarah. "Somehow."

Alaric grinned. This is it, he thought. This is my chance, my ticket to the university. All I have to do is get them to where they're going. I don't care if it's madness. I'll never have another chance like this. And if I die, at least I'll die trying.

Chapter 2

Alaric shadowed the scholars and the strange girl as they crossed the docks. The crowds made it easy to vanish in plain sight. People shouted to each other, laughed, argued, did business. They had to work to eat, just like Alaric, and there was no daylight to waste. He slipped between carts and bigger men. He lost sight of the trio once, but a quick hop onto the seawall was enough to reorient him. Lamarca, Maxime, and Zarah went directly to the Dealmaker's Pub, and Alaric followed.

Ship captains sent agents to wait in the Dealmaker. These trusted men filtered out any jobs too dangerous or cheap to be worth doing. When a good one came around, they negotiated prices and made deals.

The men in the pub knew better than to fight for work. If they tried to undercut each other, they'd all end up getting paid less. In the end, the real adversary was the one doing the hiring. Missing a job was better than taking one too cheap. More jobs would come along, but a bad loss could be fatal for a small operator.

Alaric counted to five and slipped inside.

Maxime looked around. "Do we go table to table, or do I just announce it out loud?" A few of the men in the room turned to stare at them.

"Just say it. If anyone's interested, they'll speak up," Zarah said. "I'll do it if you don't want to."

"No, no. I'll do it." Maxime shook his head and smiled. "It can't be worse than the last hour." He took a deep breath and raised his voice. "So, I have heard…. Um, pardon me. Excuse me. I have heard that this is the place to go to book passage on a ship."

He paused for a moment. A few halfhearted gazes drifted his way. "As you may have heard, a plague is ravaging our homeland of Hiberia. We are scholars from the university, and we have been seeking a cure. Our research has led us to many blocked paths and many false hopes, but we have one more that we must explore."

The dealmakers returned to their drinks.

"Well, there's simply no other way to do this," Maxime said. "I must cut to the chase and make a long story short."

"It's too late for that, Maxime," Professor Lamarca said.

"We need passage to the Isle of the World Flower in the Shrouded Sea," Maxime announced loudly.

Alaric heard a sound he'd rarely heard before: total, utter, stunned silence. The silence held for perhaps three heartbeats. Then the entire pub exploded in laughter. Loud laughter, sarcastic laughter, mocking laughter. The laughter lasted longer than the silence had. Afterward, many of the dealmakers looked less tense than they had before. But none of them replied.

Maxime raised his voice. "This is not a joke. The plague is spreading and will surely reach Thervingi soon. It may already be here. All the best minds in Hiberia seek a cure. This is madness, perhaps, but what else can we do? What can we do but go to the ends of the earth to save our people?"

"It is madness," a sailor said. "The World Flower doesn't exist. The Heaven's Tears Islands don't exist. There's nothing in the Shrouded Sea but choking mist and hidden rocks. They sink any ship that tries to sail it. Our captain isn't fool enough to take the job. Our crew isn't fool enough to do it. You won't find a man in here that will."

Another dealmaker joined in. He was dressed a bit nicer but had a nasty scar down his face. "You may find a man mad enough to take you out. You'll not find one who can bring you back alive."

"Nobody?" Maxime looked around the room. "Will no one in all of Thervingi will take us?"

"You could always go try at the Blood Bucket," the first dealmaker said. "But keep an eye on your purse when you do. And your throat."

That set off another round of laughter, not as loud as the first.

Maxime looked at his colleague, then at Zarah. "I'm sorry. I really thought we could find passage. Should we?"

"We've come this far," Lamarca said. "We can't give up now."

Alaric followed them outside. "You don't want to go to the Blood Bucket."

Lamarca jumped. "Who in the Heavenly Courts do you think you are?"

"A swindler, looking for a desperate mark," Zarah said.

"I'm no one to the Heavenly Courts," Alaric said, "but I'm trying to help. Like I said, you do not want to go to the Blood Bucket. It's not a place for honest deals. It's a den of thieves and pirates."

"Well, of course not," Maxime said, "but I don't see what choice we have. We've had no luck in the prime docks and no luck with the dealmakers. I fear this is our last resort."

"It could very well be your last anything, especially if you have your money on you." Alaric stepped a bit closer, keeping his hands where they could be seen. "They'll take your money, and then they'll take you where they want. You won't like it. You won't find any cure there. And you most likely won't come back."

"You were listening in the pub." Professor Lamarca eyed him carefully. "What do you propose?"

"How do we know you aren't trouble too?" Zarah looked down at him. She wasn't just taller than he was, but bigger. Her shoulders and back looked strong, like she spent her time moving hay bales. "How do we know that you won't take our money and leave? And don't say you're just a kid. If you're old enough to help us, you're old enough to hurt us."

"She has a point," Maxime said. "You did just follow us out of a pub. Beyond that, we know nothing."

"I followed you into a pub," Alaric said, "then back out again, without being noticed. I know these docks. I know where you shouldn't go, and I know there are more than three places to find passage."

"We know you're savvy," Lamarca said. "How do we know you're trustworthy?"

"You don't," Alaric said.

"At least you admit it," Zarah said.

"But you can trust me to act in my own best interest," Alaric said. "I'm not a captain. I don't have a ship. I'm not in a position to strand you. I make deals on the docks. I do errands. I find things for people." Alaric smiled in spite of himself. He could smell their desperation and the possibilities it held. This was his chance to make it to the university and off of these docks. "And besides, you're out of options."

"Can you find someone?" Lamarca asked.

"I know these docks better than anyone," Alaric said. "I know who's almost as desperate as you are. I know who's wild enough to take big risks. I'll find you a captain, but I need to know everything. Everything about this legend, this island, this plague, and you. Do you trust me?"

"No." Zarah turned her back on him.

"Miss Remei!" Maxime looked from Alaric to Zarah's back. "I'm sorry. I think we're leaving now. Terribly sorry. Miss Remei, why are we leaving?"

"He's lying," Zarah said. "There's no way he has a captain lined up."

"It does seem improbable," Lamarca said.

Zarah started walking. "I don't know the odds, but one look in his eyes told me all I needed to know. There is no truth in him."

"Hey!" Alaric said. "That's not true."

But Zarah kept walking, and the scholars followed, heading toward the Blood Bucket. Oh, you're not getting away that easily, Alaric thought. He gave them just enough space to not feel shadowed, then followed.

They ran into trouble before they even reached the Blood Bucket. Zarah led them directly toward it, taking them down a dim and dingy alleyway.

"Oh, come on," Alaric whispered. "Do not take that alley. Stay on the main streets. Oh, drown it all!"

"Well, look who we have here." Alaric heard the gruff voice before he reached the alley. He hurried around the corner and saw two men with knives. He'd seen them around. Yash and Onkar. They were mean enough to start all kinds of trouble, but not always smart enough to finish it.

Onkar blocked the far end of the alley like a living wall. He never said much, but his bulk and scars did the talking.

Yash dropped into the close end, boxing in the scholars. He paced and waved his arms, twitching like a heron with a brain injury. He tossed a crude knife from one hand to the other. "Two pretty girls and a soft-handed man. What are you supposed to be? Schoolteachers?" He did the talking, which was a shame. He sounded as bad as he looked.

"We are scholars from the Hiberi University," Maxime said.

"So, schoolteachers?" Onkar rumbled.

"Yes, I suppose."

"I never had much schooling," Yash said, "but it looks like I'm the smart one today. Now, what do you have for my educational fund? I can take it in coin or flesh." He waggled the knife. The constant waving almost hid his hand tremors.

Alaric stepped into the alley. "You're not half as smart as you think."

"Hey! Find your own marks, street rat!"

"I'm not looking for marks," Alaric said.

"Are you trying to rescue them? Save them? Maybe get a reward?" Yash's grating cackle joined Onkar's rumbling chuckle in sarcastic harmony.

"I'm trying to save you," Alaric said. "You used to work for Lakshi, right? You helped a friend of mine about a year ago. I'm trying to repay that."

"Huh?"

"I'm trying to help you," Alaric said slowly. "You really don't know what those robes mean, do you?"

"Yeah, we know," Yash said. "It means they're scholars. It means they have money."

"Those robes mean they're not just from the Hiberi University. Those robes mean they're from the university's royal academy."

"What does that even mean?" Yash's eyes darted from the scholars to Alaric. He waggled the knife aimlessly, like he didn't quite know who to point it at.

"It means they don't study art history," Alaric said. "It means they make weapons, poisons, and trouble. It means if you leave this alley alive, you and I are even."

"What are you talking about?"

"The Hiberi Royal Academy is the reason there are no more bandits in Hiberia," Alaric said.

"You're not really trying to help me," Yash said.

"Yash, I'm involved now," Alaric said. "I should have let them kill you. I see that now. I knew better than to stick my neck out."

"Yeah, never do that," Onkar said.

"But now I'm in this. If they burn you alive, or poison you so you cough up your lungs in little chunks, or make you convulse so hard you snap your own backbone, I'm a part of it. They can cause havoc and then walk away, but I have to live in this city."

The thin robber looked from Alaric to the scholars, his face a mask of confusion.

"Little chunks?" Onkar's deep voice got suddenly soft. "I like my lungs."

Professor Lamarca slipped her feet into a passable fighting stance, stared into the big guy's eyes, and slowly reached into her robes.

"You should take care," Maxime said. "My colleague is an expert on botanicals and chemical reactions."

"Huh?" Onkar asked.

"She knows cures and poisons and all manner of mixtures," Maxime said. "She is one of the leading experts in all of Hiberia. I would say in all of the world. Look in my eyes. I'm telling the truth."

The robbers looked from Lamarca to Maxime. "He's either telling the truth, or he's a really good liar," Yash said.

"He's telling the truth." Lamarca kept her eyes on the big man. He fidgeted and looked away. "I'm not too modest to accept the praise."

"Okay, fine. We're going. And Alaric, we're even. Whatever it was you owed me for, we're even. Come on, let's get out of here."

"Yeah, sure," Onkar said. "I like my lungs where they are."

As soon as Yash and Onkar left, a huge smile crossed Lamarca's face. "I am impressed, Alaric. And brilliant job, Maxime. I didn't know you had it in you. I knew you don't like to lie. I never thought it was because you were too good."

"I did not lie," Maxime said. "I meant every word I said."

"Well, then, you certainly weaponized the truth," Lamarca said, "and I appreciate the compliments."

"Again, I meant every word," Maxime said. "As I mean this: thank you, Alaric. I believe you saved our lives there."

"I'm glad to do it," Alaric said, "You should really consider taking my offer. These streets are dangerous. That's why I followed you."

"You have certainly proved your worth," Maxime said.

"You proved you're a fine liar," Zarah said. "Why should that make us trust you more?"

Alaric turned toward Zarah. "Is nothing enough for you? I know someone who might take you out to sea, and who won't try to knife you. I'll introduce you. How's that?"

"What's in it for you?" Lamarca asked. "If you want us to trust you, trust us."

"I want off these docks," Alaric said. "I'm smart enough to go to the university, but I don't have the money or the connections. If I make this happen for you, I want in. I want enough money to attend university. I want letters of recommendation. I want in."

Maxime looked at Professor Lamarca. "That's a lot to ask for a finding fee."

"I'll be on that ship with you all the way to the island," Alaric said. "I'll earn my way in, if you'll let me."

"Can you handle the course work?" Lamarca asked. "We can get you into the university, but we can't get you through it."

"I'm not afraid," Alaric said. "I'm good with numbers, and I remember what I hear. If I can survive out here, I can survive a classroom."

"I don't trust you," Zarah said. "You're in this for yourself. You don't care about us or this plague. I can see it in your eyes."

"I told you why I'm doing this," Alaric said. "I can help you, and then the professors can help me."

"You can't help us." Zarah stared into Alaric's eyes. "You don't have a ship, and there is no truth in you. You even lie to yourself."

Alaric shivered. "I don't. I know how long my odds are. I know how far I'll have to go. I…I can get you a ship. I know someone who will take you." Even as he spoke, Alaric realized the girl had a point. He had a lead, but he'd sold it to them—and himself—as a sure bet. "I'll make this happen."

"Perhaps we should listen to him," Maxime said. "We are quickly running out of options."

Zarah shook her head. "He doesn't even know how false he is. He can't be true to us. We'd be better off with a liar than with a fool who believes his own tales." She and Lamarca walked away. Maxime hesitated with an apologetic grimace, then followed.

"No!" Alaric shouted. "No! You will not walk away into another death trap. I'm not going to watch you all get shanked because this girl doesn't trust me."

Zarah spun around and stepped toward Alaric. "This girl is the reason we're here." Her pale face flushed with anger as she stared down at him. She had shoulders like a dockworker, and she squared off with him. "This girl is going to reach the Isle of the World Flower if it kills her. And this girl isn't going to be taken in by a scoundrel who doesn't even know his own truth."

"You think you're better than I am?" Alaric had faced down much bigger, armed men many times. He'd be drowned if he let a girl his own age intimidate him. "You think you're so perfectly honest? You think you're so far above me you can't even let me help you after I saved your life?"

"Honest?" Zarah laughed a barking expulsion of breath that held more anger than humor. "Honest? You are the third person I've told about the plants. The professors are the first two. That's it. I knew when it first started that no one would believe me. I knew they'd think I was mad. So, I hid it from everyone for my entire life. I haven't even told my parents. I love my parents, but I haven't told them anything."

"Oh," Alaric whispered. Zarah's size didn't scare him, but the ferocity in her green eyes did. He felt like he was staring into the heart of the angry sea.

"So, yes, I've been hiding the most important part of me all my life, but at least I know I'm lying. At least I know what I'm hiding. And I try to tell the truth about everything else," Zarah said. "But you? You just say whatever you want to be true and hope you can make it happen somehow."

"That's not—"

"You spin the truth so much," Zarah said, "you're too dizzy to know what's real and what's made up."

Alaric felt his face burn red with rage and embarrassment. "You don't know me." His voice was as tight as a garotte wire. "You don't know my life. You grew up on a farm, with food and a bed every night, enough room for you and all the voices in your head. You haven't told your parents your little secret? I haven't told my parents anything, ever, because I never knew them. You don't know what I've had to do to survive, and you don't get to judge me for it."

"You're right," Zarah said softly. "I don't know your life, and I have no right to judge you. But I do have to decide whether or not I trust you with my life. And more than my life, with my call and my mission, and the lives of all the people this cure could save." She bit her lip. "And I hate to say it, but you're still spinning. What you said was true. It felt true. But it didn't have anything to do with what we are talking about."

"What?"

"We were talking about whether or not we could trust you, not whether or not you were justified in lying. That's two different things, and I think you're old enough to know it." Her expression had softened. The sea in her eyes had stilled but remained as deep and vast as before.

Alaric forced himself to look into Zarah's eyes. If he looked away, even an inch, he'd lose his nerve and spin the truth again. "You want my truth? I don't want money or power or fame. I want respect. I want to earn those robes because I'm smart enough, yes, but also because no one can buy or inherit those robes. No one can pay their way through. The richest man still has to pass the classes, write the papers, do the work. No one could ever look down on me again. That's what I want."

"That's a lot closer to the truth." A surprised smile crossed Zarah's face, and she looked suddenly bashful and somehow pretty.

"That is the truth, at least as I understand it." Alaric stumbled over his words for a moment, then collected himself. "You know my price. Do you want my help or not?"

"I know you don't trust him," Lamarca said, "but we're in over our heads. This is too dangerous. Let him try."

"I concur," Maxime said. "If he fails, we'll go straight to the Blood Bucket. I promise."

"I'll trust you for now," Zarah said. "But I'm keeping my eyes on you. You may not know truth from tales, but I do."

Alaric smiled. "I wouldn't have it any other way. Come on. We won't find Captain Crimson here among the filth."

Chapter 3

Alaric led Zarah and the professors up the steep hill to Port Theron's financial district.

"Why are you taking us away from the docks?" Zarah asked. "We need a ship, not a bank."

"We're looking for a captain, not a boat," Alaric answered.

The city smelled of many things: sea water, decaying seaweed, coal smoke, horse dung. Alaric scarcely noticed them. They faded into the scrum of daily life like the sounds of hungry seagulls, hurried footsteps, and hard voices. But a new smell cut through the haze. Alaric breathed deep. A big smile crossed his face. "Coffee."

"Coffee?" Zarah sniffed the air and grimaced. "We don't have time to stop for coffee. We're trying to stop a plague. Or is this part of your plan? Where are you taking us?"

"The Hawk and Bean," Alaric said. "Port Theron's best coffeehouse."

"Why?" Zarah asked.

"Small deals get made on the docks," Alaric said. "Big deals get made uptown. And this journey is quite a big deal." He grinned. "Also, I like coffee. Especially when someone else is buying."

Maxime gestured at the Hawk and Bean's well-polished dark wood interior and brass railings and fittings. "This is nicer than the Dealmaker. I approve." Men in business suits sat with women in fine dresses. Two officers of the Thervingi Navy sat with a ship captain from one of the merchant companies. A man in Bosphori royal livery joined them.

"Coffee's expensive." Alaric caught the barista's eye, held up four fingers, and then led the scholars to a table. "It's the one luxury I allow myself, and that rarely."

"Will we be able to talk privately?" Lamarca asked. The table they sat at was right in the middle of everything. "There are a lot of people here."

"Everybody minds their own business here."

Maxime smiled. "The less secretive we look, the more anonymity we'll have. This is a bit like going home."

"You grew up in a coffeehouse?" Zarah asked.

Maxime laughed. "I grew up rich. We like our privacy. I'm the younger son of a baron."

"You're nobility, and you went through all the work to become a scholar?" Zarah asked.

"I understand Alaric a bit more than you think," Maxime said. "A nobleman's younger son is always just a spare heir unless he finds a way to earn his path. I didn't want to buy a spot in the naval officers academy. I have no interest in killing or dying violently. But I do love to learn. And I had to earn these robes."

"I bet your parents are proud," Zarah said. "You didn't have to do any of this."

Maxime laughed. "Not really. They think I'm living beneath my station. But at least I respect myself."

"Maybe you do get me, a little," Alaric said. "We'll have privacy here. People this rich don't spy. They hire people like me to spy for them. Now, before we continue, the deal still stands. You get your island, and I get to study at the university. You find a way to pay for my tuition, books, living expenses, and the hidden fees I don't even know about. In return, I help you save the world."

Zarah laughed. "We sound ridiculous when you say it like that."

"I'm not laughing," Alaric said. "You're either mad, or you're carrying thousands of lives on your shoulders."

"Oh." Zarah smiled weakly. "Good thing I have big shoulders."

"The deal stands," Maxime said. "I'll pay your way myself if it comes to that. You'll be able to attend."

"Good," Alaric said. "It's time Zarah tells her tale. I need to know everything before I agree to my end."

"I thought you wanted this job," Zarah said. "You worked awfully hard to get us to trust you."

"I wanted the opportunity," Alaric said, "but I'm not going to throw my life away. If this is impossible, or suicide, I'm not going. Even if I survive, it's no good to me if Maxime and Lamarca don't. They can't get me into the university if they're dead. And I can't go if I'm dead."

"I see my death doesn't weigh in," Zarah said.

Alaric shrugged.

"I'll start," Lamarca said. "My field is botany. I research plants as medicine. Every professor in our university is working to cure this plague, but we have nothing. No vaccine, no treatment, not even a palliative to ease the symptoms."

"The plague is spreading quickly," Maxime said. "It kills nearly one in ten. The death count is already in the hundreds. It will surge to the thousands or tens of thousands if we do not find a solution quickly. I'm not sure where it will stop, or how many it could kill. Our prince tried to close the borders, but we were able to slip through."

"I've spent weeks focused on this one problem," Lamarca said. "I've put aside my other research. I've neglected social commitments. I've given up more hours of sleep than I can easily count. We all have, but we've still got nothing. We're not going to fix this in the lab."

Alaric whistled. "That is quite the context."

"We've exhausted all rational avenues, but hope brings us here."

A young woman arrived with four steaming cups of dark coffee. Alaric lifted his cup gently toward his face and breathed deep. The rich, complex aromas filled his senses. There were subtle notes in good coffee for those who knew how to look for them. In this cup, he smelled a faint floral sweetness and a woodsy, earthy smell like oak barrels.

"This is good," he told the waitress. "Is this a new blend?"

"It is," she said. "We got some new beans in from south of Kartargo. The brewmaster roasts them dark…well, I can't tell you everything, can I?"

Alaric smiled. "Even if you did, I couldn't reproduce a blend this fine. Maxime, tip well."

Maxime paid the waitress, and she left. "I've had some prestigious publications in the area of mythology and folklore," he said. "Are you familiar with the legend of the Shrouded Sea and the Heaven's Tears?"

"Not particularly." Alaric kept his coffee cup in front of his face while he said it, pretending to be focused on the aromas and flavors. "Part of the Southern Sea is permanently shrouded in mist. Some believe there are islands within the fog, full of mysteries and treasures. Most of us think that it's just mist and rocks. No one comes back rich. Most don't come back at all."

Alaric took a sip of coffee, hoping nobody had seen through the lie. He'd heard songs. He'd heard stories. He'd never thought they were real, but he remembered them all.

"You may be right," Maxime said. "It may be a fool's errand. But it is our best hope."

"It's not much of a hope then," Alaric said. "Even if this island exists, who could find it?"

"If you two will stop running your mouths for a minute, I'll tell you." Zarah took a sip of her coffee and made a face. "You really like this stuff?"

"It tastes bitter and ugly at first," Alaric said, "but if you keep drinking it, you learn to really taste it. There's a lot more there underneath. You just have to learn how to find it." He smiled. "I was wondering where you fit into this."

"The World Flower's calling me. I can find it. I can guide us to it. I can guide a ship to it. All I have to do is listen."

"That's a lot to believe." Alaric looked at Zarah across his coffee cup. "Convince me."

Zarah took a deep breath. "Plants have talked to me for as long as I can remember. First it was just the ones in our garden. They would tell me when they needed more water, or when the weeds threatened them. It was nice. Eventually, I started hearing all the fields and forests around me, like the noise of a crowd. It surrounds you, but you can't really hear anything, like the people here. About a month ago, one voice cut through the crowd."

"The World Flower?" Alaric asked.

"Yes." Zarah raised her head defiantly, daring him to question her. "The World Flower calls me. It will not be ignored. At first, I thought I was going mad, but when the plague broke out, it all made sense. The World Flower is calling me, guiding me, to the cure. I can lead us there. I can save the world."

Alaric leaned across the table. "You're insane. This is madness."

Zarah lunged forward and grabbed his wrists. "Look me in the eye and say that again."

Alaric looked down at his wrists. "Let me go."

"Look in my eyes and say that again."

Alaric looked up. Zarah's eyes seemed to glow green. "I said, you're insane. This is...."

His words trailed off as the world faded away.

Alaric ran along the jungle path, ducking throat-choking vines and face-lashing branches. His breath burned in his lungs, his blood pounded in his ears, and the sweltering heat plastered his clothes to his body. A thousand smells filled the air: the perfume of flowers, driven by the heat, floral, the thick sap of vines, the wetness of new growth, and something terrible underneath, something sad and angry and unspeakably old.

He kept his eyes on the ground, struggling to keep his feet from tangling in the net of vines and roots that covered the ground. One false step could send him sprawling with a twisted ankle. And then he couldn't run anymore. He dared not look back at them, but he could feel them drawing closer.

The path led upward, around and around in wide circle. He grabbed hold of a branch to steady himself, but the smooth bark beneath his hand peeled away like paper. He jerked his hand back as a foul, caustic-smelling sap dripped out.

The hand he drew back had long, strong fingers, light skin, and thick calluses. It was not his own. "Zarah?"

Alaric glanced over his shoulder. He had to see if they were still following.

They were. Five skeletal, twisted forms lurched forward, made not of bone, but of thick, knotted vines with thorns jutting in every direction. They moved like men—almost. Long, jabbing thorns grew where their fingers should have been. Thorns that could drive through his body and leave him bleeding out. Thorns that could rip through his flesh and tear out his heart itself.

He turned and ran again. He burst through the canopy of leaves and found himself a hundred feet above a crashing sea. He clung tight to the vines, his feet kicking against the edge. Mist veiled the ocean, hiding the horizon in a wall of white. He looked over his shoulder.

The thorn men had stopped moving. They stood awaiting orders, trying to figure out who and what he was.

"Come, little one, brave the Shrouded Sea and find me." The voice filled the jungle, reaching into the cooler sea air, as if it were coming from every plant at once, or from the earth itself. "Find me and reach me, and you shall have what you seek. You shall have life if you can claim it. Come, Zarah, and find what you seek." The voice paused. "Alaric, I know you. Come. Help little Zarah find her way."

"Will I find what I seek?" Alaric heard the words, but he wasn't sure he'd spoken them.

"I give you no promises," the voice said, "only a call."

The thorn men began approaching, staggering ever closer, cutting off his only path of escape. Nowhere to run. He glanced at the skeletal vines, then out at the sea. It was too far to fall. He'd be crushed against the rocks below. And if he somehow survived the fall, the churning water would drive him under and drown him.

"Rot and corruption stand against you. Pain and decay threaten every step. But if you can reach me, the healing will begin, and all will be set to right."

The twisted thorn forms lurched toward him, their barbed fingers outstretched, a hollow hunger where their eyes should be. Alaric looked back at the water and thought it would at least be a better death.

He closed his eyes and jumped.

Alaric came back to himself with a great gasping breath. Zarah let go of his wrists, and he fell back into his chair with a crash. He looked all around the coffeehouse, unsure what, if any of it, was real.

"What was that? I was—" Alaric gasped. "I was you. Where … where were we?"

"The Isle of the World Flower," Zarah said. "Do you still think I'm mad?"

Alaric shuddered. "You're mad to want to go there."

Zarah smirked. "I don't have much choice. I'm the only one who can. The question is, will you help us?"

Alaric raised his coffee to his mouth and took a few slow breaths. The steam and the rich, sharp scent steadied him.

"This is real. This is still madness, and it might be suicide, but it's real. I'm in."

Chapter 4

Alaric sat back in his chair, staring at Zarah. The vision hung around the edges of his perception like the morning mists, blurring the world until the sun burned them away. The lush, overwhelming smell of sap and flowers slowly gave way to the smell of roasting coffee. The cool mist of the island slowly gave way to the crowded heat of the coffeehouse. The inhuman hunger of the thorn men lingered in the back of his mind, though he knew they were half a world away.

"It's real," he whispered. "Some part of it all—gods, the Heavenly Court, the Creator—something's actually real. It might want us dead, but it's real."

"A skeptic," Maxime said. "I can sympathize."

"I never believed any of it," Alaric said. "The Heavenly Court, their priests and temples, the High King of Heaven, much less the legends of the Heaven's Tears Islands in the Shrouded Sea. I thought it was all just fancy names and tall tales to get people to visit the temples. But some of it isn't. Something's real."

"It's a lot to take in," Zarah said. "I wasn't even skeptical before. But there's a big difference between thinking all that is out there somewhere and realizing something divine knows your name."

Alaric shuddered. "Well, I know you're not lying."

"Will you help us find a captain?" Maxime asked.

Alaric took another long drink of his coffee, pouring the bitter, lukewarm dregs down his throat. "I know somebody who might help us. She's brave, smart, and greedy. She might just say yes. She's a bit of a legend in these parts."

"A woman sea captain?" Maxime said. "Good. She won't think it's bad luck to sail with women."

"Can you find her?" Lamarca said.

Alaric smiled and looked across the coffeehouse. "That's the other reason I brought you here. I like coffee. But Captain Jill Crimson loves it. Almost as much as she loves gold. Come with me. She'll be in the back room, playing mak-lom."

Alaric led the scholars and Zarah to the back of the coffee shop.

"Why have we stopped?" Maxime looked around. "I don't see her or anyone else back here."

Alaric pushed a section of wall. It swung open easily.

"A secret door?"

"Not secret, just discrete." Alaric stepped inside and pointed at a mak-lom table. A half-dozen spectators watched a well-dressed man lay a black stone on the board. They all breathed in as he did, leaning just a bit closer. On the table were two stacks of silver coins, each coin a week's wage for a laborer.

The sea captain sat at the head of the table, a tall mug of coffee in one hand, a round red stone in the other. Her dark hair fell in curls across her shoulders, like waves crashing against a rocky shore. Dark brown eyes twinkled from a cool brown face. From the red tricorn hat atop her head to the red leather boots on her feet, she looked like an actor playing a role. Yet somehow, the gleam in her eyes and the predatory grin on her face said she owned the entire city.

"She's magnificent," Maxime said. "Like a cat in a throne room, she doesn't care what anyone else thinks."

"It was a pleasure taking your money, chap." Captain Jill Crimson laid the red stone down on the table. The onlookers let out their collective breath. Before anyone, even the loser, could really get angry, the captain held up a coin and told the waiter on duty, "A round on me." Then she slid both piles of coins into her coin purse.

A few moments later, the waiter hurried in with a tray of steaming mugs and began handing them out.

She caught Alaric's eye. "Who says money can't buy happiness? They look happy to me."

The men gathered around the game table dispersed to give the captain some room. Jill walked toward Alaric.

"Perhaps it's only other people's money that can buy happiness," Alaric said, "in which case we may be about to make you happy."

"I don't know you, kid, but I knew you had business in mind when I saw you," the captain said, "unless you've come to lose at stones too."

"We need more than a lesson in humility," Alaric said. "We need a captain who's willing to go off the charted lanes."

Jill gestured to a table in the corner of the room. "Boys, you'll have to play a few rounds without me."

"We need to go off the maps, to the Shrouded Sea. I'll tell you more if you're interested."

"The Shrouded Sea?" Captain Crimson's eyebrows rose. "That's impossible."

"We're hoping the island we need will be on its near edge," Alaric said. "We have a navigator. Miss Remei knows how to find it."

"Is this true, girl?" The captain's dark eyes narrowed. "Don't let this boy chart a course you can't sail."

Zarah nodded. "If you get me to the Shrouded Sea, I can get you through it."

Jill stared at Zarah as the wall clock ticked and their coffee slowly cooled. In the end, she had only one question. "How much?"

Maxime pulled three small purses from different locations within his clothing. He opened them just enough to show the gems and gold inside.

The captain looked through them all. "That's it?"

"I have a fourth purse with a few small coins for meals and other incidentals. Altogether it's not worth one of these coins."

"It's not enough."

"It's all I have with me. It's a lot of money." Maxime looked at Alaric, Zarah, and Lamarca with an almost defensive expression on his face. "It really is a lot of money. It's everything I had saved, and some of what I could get from my family." He looked down at his hand and slid his ring from his finger. "What if I add this? It's real gold and real sapphires. The workmanship is…." He paused and took a deep breath. "This has been in my family for over a hundred years. The workmanship is irreplaceable."

"Keep your family jewels." Jill pushed the ring back to him. "Even with the ring, it's not close. This would be enough for a safe trip, but to go off the maps? That's dangerous, and dangerous is expensive. And the Shrouded Sea is more than dangerous; it's madness, and madness is very expensive."

"We have a good reason," Zarah said. "A plague is sweeping Hiberia. You know it will reach Thervingi. You know it will reach everywhere."

The captain's eyes grew wide for a moment, then she laughed quietly. "You think you'll find a cure out there in the mists of the Shrouded Sea? You think what you need is just waiting for you to go claim it?"

"Yes," Zarah said.

She looked at the four of them and shook her head. "It's clear none of you have ever been to sea before. You've no idea how dangerous it is. A voyage to uncharted waters is perilous enough. We won't know what dangers we'll face. We won't know whether we'll find resources for repairs, or even fresh water to drink. But to go into a mist-shrouded sea? To sail blind? Literally blind? That's not just dangerous. That's reckless and foolish. That's madness."

"I can get us there." Zarah stood. "If you get me to the edge of the Shrouded Sea, I can steer your ship to the Isle of the World Flower."

"How?" Jill stood in response. Zarah was a bit taller, but the captain owned the space.

"The World Flower's been calling me for weeks, ever since the plague began. It calls me in my dreams. It calls me every waking hour. It's calling now. It wants me to reach it. I need to reach it. And all I need is a ship and a crew."

"And…my price just went up." Jill tilted her head and smirked until Zarah's cheeks flushed red, and her wide eyes rimmed with tears. "Sit down, girl. It's bad enough you want to go into the mists. But you think you'll actually find the Isle of the World Flower? You think it actually exists? You think it's calling you? You think it wants to give you the cure? Even if I wanted to, my crew would never buy into such a mad quest. Not for this little." Her smirk turned to a frown, and Alaric thought he saw the hint of disappointment in her eyes.

"What about the treasure?" Alaric said.

"The treasure?" Jill raised one eyebrow. "What treasure?"

"You're a sea captain," Alaric said. "I'm sure you've heard as many shanties and old sailor's tales as I have. You've heard The Ballad of Captain Valens."

"I have." The captain's smile showed her teeth, straight and pale yellow, one capped in gold. "I heard it from an old Bosphori sailor who'd heard it from his great-grandfather. I know a few verses the world forgot."

"Then you know about the treasure of the Heaven's Tears. You've heard about how Valens found his way through the mists. They say he buried his greatest treasure on the Isle of the World Flower, thinking no one could ever find it again." Alaric grinned, pressing the point. "And he was right. No one was able to find it, not even Valens himself. He went back for it but never returned. His treasure still waits out there. Think about it. Chests full of rare gems, taken from every raid and plunder of his career."

"You think there's any truth in that old tale?" Crimson asked.

"Until I met Zarah Remei, I didn't think the Isle of the World Flower existed. I didn't think there was anything in the Shrouded Sea except riptides, reefs, and rocks. I thought the fog and the dangerous waters were the reason no one ever came back. And with no mystical island, there was no reason to believe a word of that old sailor's tale. But now? Now that we have a way to find the Isle of the World Flower? If the island is real, why not the treasure, too?"

The captain stared into Alaric's eyes for a few moments.

"Come on, Captain Crimson, I know your reputation. I can see it in your eyes. You want this. You want to go where no one else has gone. You want to find what no one else can find. You want to cure a plague no one else can cure."

Jill nodded. "I think I can sell this to my crew. Even split fifty ways, that treasure would make us all as rich as kings."

"Fifty-two," Alaric said.

"Fifty-two?"

"Fifty-two. The captain always gets two shares, right?"

"Yes, and I'm the captain."

"And I'll be taking my two shares, as well," Alaric said. "I'm the one who brought you this job. I brought you the one person who can lead you to the island and the treasure. I'm coming along, and I'm taking my share."

Jill laughed. "The depths you are."

Alaric smiled. "Your eyes are already shining like the diamonds Captain Valens hid. I can see it in your face. The quest is in your head. You want the pride, the reputation, and the respect. You want to be the only captain in the world who could bring in that legendary treasure. And more than that, you want to see the island. You want to see what's out there hidden in the mists."

"You're right," the captain said, "but I know something too. You went to the docks and the Dealmaker before you came here. If I say no, you're left with the cutthroats at the Blood Bucket."

"Maybe," Alaric said, "but here's the strange thing. When one person wants something, it becomes wanted. If you want the job, but we walk away, what next? We're not alone in here. Word will get out. How many other captains might come calling then? One of them will give us our share."

"Drown you, boy! I won't underestimate you again." Jill poured the remains of her lukewarm coffee down her throat, then wiped her face with the back of her hand. "You've got a deal. Meet me at my ship tomorrow morning. The Scarlet Gray, common docks berth thirteen. Be there at dawn."

Alaric grinned. "We'll be there nice and early, but you won't sail without us."

"You might be surprised," Captain Crimson said. "I'm a captain, not a king. My crew has to agree to the bargain, and you'll have to convince them."

Chapter 5

"That went better than expected." Alaric led them out of the back room and into the hallway. Thick wooden walls muted the low rumble from the conversations in the main room and silenced the sounds of gambling in the back. From back here, they could smell the next batch of beans roasting. Alaric breathed deep and smiled. "Captain Jill Crimson wants this job. I'm sure we can convince her crew."

"You didn't say anything about a treasure," Zarah whispered.

Alaric shrugged. "It probably doesn't exist. But the hope of finding it will get the crew on board."

"That's worse!" Zarah said. "You're lying to them so they'll risk their lives for us."

"I'm telling them about a possibility," Alaric said. "And risking their lives is exactly what you want them to do. This is your quest, your call, your magic flower."

"That doesn't matter," Zarah said. "You should have told us about the treasure before we met the captain. I told you everything I'm going through, as mad as it all sounds, and you just sat on a secret treasure and didn't bother telling us?"

"I didn't think you cared about money," Alaric said.

"We don't!" Zarah sputtered. She looked at the scholars and waved her hands.

"I believe Miss Remei is saying, quite correctly, that this treasure changes our entire dynamic," Maxime said.

Alaric raised one eyebrow. "I still want to be a scholar. Why are you upset that I might get rich too? Did you want me to be your charity case? Did you want to keep me dependent on you? That's not how I operate."

"You say you want to become a scholar, and I believe you do," Lamarca said, "but I was listening. Really listening. What you want is worth and respect, the kind you can only earn, but the kind that everyone can see. You want to something that proves to everyone—including you—that you've done it, you deserve it."

Alaric frowned. "That cuts a little deep."

"The university is one path," Lamarca said. "War is another, but you're not a killer. There aren't many others. Birth and bloodlines still dominate our world. But this treasure? It's a big one. You'd be rich and powerful, much more than any scholar."

"Wealth proves nothing," Alaric said. "Some of the most worthless people I know are wealthy."

"You're doing it again," Zarah said. "Do you even realize you're telling half-truths?"

"You wouldn't just be rich," Lamarca said. "You'd be one of the men who found Captain Valens's legendary treasure. Sailors, pirates, and soldiers have sought it for decades. Many never returned. None found it. But if you were part of the crew that did, you'd be a legend. You wouldn't have to tell a half-truth then. And you wouldn't need our university, or us."

"You think I'll abandon you if I find the treasure?" Alaric said.

"Will you?" Zarah asked.

Alaric frowned. "Rich men don't like plagues either."

"That's not an answer."

"You want me to predict the future?" Alaric asked. "You want a promise? You want me to go to the Temple of Truth and swear on their altar? You think that would be worth the coins it would cost?"

"I'd like an honest answer," Zarah said. "Precious hope of that."

"I know what you're trying to do is important," Alaric said. "I'll do what I can to help you, even if I've already found the treasure. But don't ask me to die for you or give up everything. I'm your guide, not your brother."

"You're only our guide if the crew says yes," Zarah said.

"We'll find out in the morning," Alaric said. "Do you have a place to stay?"

"We have two rooms at the Gull's Feather Inn," Maxime said. "You're welcome to stay with me if you want to get an early start."

"I have things to do before I leave town," Alaric said. "Meet me outside just before dawn. And be ready."

Alaric stood outside the Gull's Feather Inn, waiting on Maxime, Lamarca, and Zarah. The cool of the morning offered little in Thervingi, just a respite from the blanket of wet heat that covered the days.

He stole glances toward the sea and toward the east. Clouds dampened the dawn, muting blue to gray and gold to pale yellow, but today's sunrise shone brighter and held more promise than yesterday's, at least to Alaric.

"Ah, good! I see you're on time." Maxime held the door for Lamarca and Zoe.

"Where's your luggage?" Alaric asked.

"We're traveling light," Lamarca said. "We had to sneak across the Hiberi border to get here."

"A porter is taking our bags to the ship," Maxime said. "Pitifully few bags, for such a long trip. I'm not accustomed to traveling light."

"Let's get going." Alaric motioned for them to follow. "The Scarlet Gray, berth thirteen, common docks. I know the way." He led them downhill through the maze of streets and alleys toward the common docks.

"I hope the crew accepts the job," Maxime said. "They seem to be our last resort."

"They will," Alaric said, "and if they don't, I'll find a crew that will. I know these docks. You're safe with me."

"Look who we have here!" a voice said. The big Vorali from yesterday. He cracked his knuckles. His shorter companion stood beside him. "The little brat who got away. You helping more strays? What are you? Charity?"

Alaric tensed, then turned to face the men. "You here for another taste of pepper dust? I know you Vorali don't season your food, but there are better ways to get some flavor."

"Yesterday, you cost us a lot of money." The shorter thug ran his fingers through his graying ginger hair. "Today, we're going to take it out of your hide."

"I saved both of your lives," Alaric said. "Lennick was carrying for Lakshi. You think he'd let you rob his courier and live?"

"We're not afraid of Lakshi," the big guy said. "Do you know who we work for?"

"Dughall's got half the territory and half the men Lakshi has. He wouldn't risk a war he can't win. Not for a couple of goons like you," Alaric said. "You've got no skills. You'd be replaced before your bodies grew cold."

The smaller thug smirked. Angry pink skin wrinkled around pale blue eyes. "Good thing you don't work for Lakshi."

Alaric shoved Maxime forward. "Run!"

The scholar stumbled two steps, then started running. Lamarca kept pace with her colleague. Zarah's heavy footsteps thudded behind them.

Alaric glanced over his shoulder. The two thugs ran after them, red faced and raging.

"What do they want with you?" Zarah shouted.

"I saved a kid from getting robbed, maybe worse. Left here!" Alaric took the corner easily. Maxime and Lamarca skidded.

Zarah nearly slammed into the alley wall. "Oof! Why would they rob a kid?"

"Because it's easy." Alaric's blood pounded in his ears. Sweat covered him, despite the cool of the morning. "No more questions! Follow me." He looked all around for an escape.

"Why aren't we in public?" Maxime struggled to breathe. The question came out as a croak. "Surely, they…surely…."

"We're in Dughall's territory. Crowds won't matter," Alaric said.

"Then how do we escape?"

"We turn two corners, and we lose them," Alaric said. "Now, no more questions!" He led them out of the alley onto what should have been a busy street. Instead, the street had been cleared for a building crew adding onto the East Bosphor Joint Stock Company's office. "Keep running! This way."

He dragged them around another corner into an alleyway.

"We're heading back the way we came," Zarah said.

"Street's blocked. Hurry—oh no."

The big Vorali thug stepped into the far side of the alley. "Thought you could get away from us."

His partner stepped in from the others side. "Unlike you, we knew the street would be closed."

"You might be faster," the big thug said, "but we're smarter."

"Somehow, I doubt that," Lamarca said. She leaned over and took a deep breath.

"Do you think the…gasp…scholar bluff…will work again?" Maxime said. His face was almost as red as those of the thugs.

"Not after you said that," Lamarca said.

"Not after we ran," Alaric said. "Be ready."

The big thug walked toward Alaric. "Hey, you think we should let these guys go?"

"They look rich," his partner said. "We should at least rob them."

"Yeah, yeah. I told you we were smart." The big guy loomed over Alaric. "After we smash this little dock rat."

Alaric stared into the red-faced man's eyes.

The big Vorali laughed. "What? Acting tough? Trying to stare me down?"

Alaric slowly reached his hand down to his belt. He closed his hand around the pepper packet, waiting for just the right moment. "I'm just mesmerized by your eyes. They're so pale, and ugly, and completely devoid of intelligence."

He flung his hand upward, but the thug grabbed his wrist.

"That won't work this time, little man." The big Vorali squeezed with his left hand and drew back his right for a heavy punch. "This is gonna hurt."

Suddenly, Zarah lunged forward, shoving Alaric to the side. He spun around the pivot point of his wrist, still held tight in the big man's grip.

Zarah's left hand drove into the thug's liver with a loud smack. The big man's hand released. His pale eyes watered. His knees wobbled, and he almost fell to the ground.

"Hey!" The older thug shoved past the two scholars, his face twisting in rage and shock.

Alaric smashed the pepper packet into his face. A fine dust of ashes and hot pepper powder exploded around the thug's head, filling his nose and eyes. He gasped and choked, clawing at his face.

"Run!" Alaric shouted. "They won't be down long!"

They raced toward the docks, leaving the two thugs sputtering and staggering far behind them.

When they reached the edge of the common docks, Alaric stopped. "We can catch our breath now. Zarah, where did you learn to hit like that?"

Zarah stared. "Look at me, boy. I'm half a head taller and twice as thick as you. Why wouldn't I hit hard?"

"You almost dropped a very big man," Maxime said. "It was unexpected, even to me."

Zarah shrugged. "I live on a farm. We take care of things ourselves. A sheep gets stuck somewhere, you pull her out. Wall needs new rocks, you carry them. Hay needs baling, you bale it. An ugly thug needs punching, you punch him."

"That was quite a punch," Lamarca said. "Thank you."

"Yeah," Alaric said. "Thanks." He took a deep breath. "Well, we're here. Berth thirteen, the Scarlet Gray. Our trouble should be over now."

"If we can convince the crew to accept the task," Maxime said.

"You'd better hope we can, Alaric," Zarah said, "because you are becoming a problem. Those thugs were after you. Your enemies almost stopped us before we even started."

"Miss Remei," Maxime said, "please. We knew this city was dangerous—"

"That danger was not our own," Zarah said. "It was his. Alaric, if we don't leave on that ship, I'm done with you. My mission is too important to fail because of you."

Chapter 6

"Welcome to the Scarlet Gray." Captain Jill Crimson stood at the gangplank, tall and grand in her red hat, belt, coat, and boots. The east glowed gold, and the sky overhead shone bright blue. Seagulls rode the sea winds, crying back and forth. The salt of the sea pushed the city's smells back, cleaning and sharpening the air. "I'll introduce you to my crew."

They would not be the first ship out this morning. Already the prime docks had nearly emptied. The remaining ships had all made it to the launch buoys, pulled by warp-rope. One by one, they let the ebbing tide push them into open water. From there, their sails caught the wind, and they leapt into motion.

"This is my boatswain, Callum Westwind." The name and fair skin told Alaric that Callum was from Vorali, the most northern of the Six Nations. Alaric frowned. The boatswain looked like the men he'd just escaped from.

"Pleased to meet you," Alaric said.

"The same," Callum said.

"My quartermaster, Hannibal Three-Fingers."

A tall Kartargan man with a shaved head, alert brown eyes, and deep brown skin raised his right hand. The ring and smallest finger were missing. "Welcome aboard."

"Rook, where's my first mate?" the captain asked.

A stout Thervingi with graying hair jolted. "Huh?" He looked around for a moment as if thinking of an excuse. "He's aboard somewhere. I just saw him."

Jill laughed. "Waiting for the best time to make an entrance, no doubt. We'll start. He'll be here when he's needed. He always is." She turned to address her crew. "Sailors, we have a job offer. But this is no simple cargo haul. If we take this job, we'll sail the open seas, and pierce the mists of the Shrouded Sea to find a mythical island. Our patrons seek a cure for the coming plague, and also the treasure of Captain Valens. It's a fool's mission, but if we succeed, we'll be the world's richest heroes."

Gasps and mutters crossed the deck of the ship.

"We are a crew. We live as a crew. We face down Lord Death as a crew. We make decisions like this as a crew," Jill said. "So now, you will hear what I heard. Ask questions. Argue. Press for answers. Then we will decide." She nodded toward the scholars. "You have the deck."

Professor Lamarca stepped forward. "You've heard rumors of a plague in the north." She paused, and the crew nodded or gave noises of assent. "It's worse than you think. It's spreading quickly, killing nearly one in ten. They've already closed the borders. We had to sneak out of Hiberia just to get here."

"Why did you come here?" Callum said, "and why does this concern us?"

"Our university has dropped everything else to find a cure or treatment," Lamarca said. "We've closed classes, shelved other research, and all but given up on sleeping. We've got nothing to show for it. Almost nothing. Maxime?"

"Professor Lamarca is an expert on plants, chemicals, and medicines," Maxime said. "My field is history and folklore. At first, I thought there was nothing I could do to help stop this plague. But I decided to see if anything like this had ever happened before. I found one old legend—centuries old—from the time of warring clans and small kingdoms. 'Seek the World Flower on its island in the Shrouded Sea, and you will find your cure.'"

"What about the treasure?" Hannibal asked.

"You've all heard tell of Captain Valens's treasure," Alaric said. "He stole it from his own crew. For ten years, he hid the best jewels before he divided the treasure."

"Yeah, that's why they killed him," Rook said.

"Right," Alaric said. "When his crew found out, they turned against him. But before they mutinied, he hid the treasure. You know the story, right?"

"But his crew spent the rest of their lives searching for it and never found it," Rook said. "Many of them died trying. Since then, people have looked everywhere."

"Everywhere except the Shrouded Sea," Alaric said. "It's the one place the treasure would be safe. Some of the legends said Captain Valens hid his treasure on the very island we're looking for. The Isle of the World Flower."

"I heard those songs too," Rook said, "but I don't know about this. It's a great treasure if we find it. I think we're more likely to end up crashed against the rocks. But I'm with the crew. If we decide to go, I'm in. I'll do my part."

Captain Crimson smiled. "You always do, Rook Corbin."

Callum laughed. "That treasure never existed outside the daydreams of drunken sailors. I don't want to die for a fairytale."

"Let's say this island is real." Hannibal said it like he was telling a joke, but then turned suddenly serious. "Do we know how far it is? Will we have enough food and fresh water to make it there and back again? Don't tell me we will just resupply on this magical island."

A murmur went through the crew.

"Starvation is a greater terror than violent death," Hannibal said. "You can fight back against an attacker, and if you lose, your death is quick. Starvation and thirst are slow, cruel killers, and no blade nor bullet can lay them low."

"I know it's dangerous," Lamarca said, "but so is staying here. This plague won't stay in Hiberia. It will reach Thervingi soon enough, then Bosphor, Kartargo, and even Solok. This is our chance to find a cure, to save our world. It's dangerous, but it's worth it." She looked out across the crew. A few of the sailors nodded along. A few were even moved to stand. But it wasn't enough.

"This isn't a fairy tale," Zarah said. "We're not just chasing a line from an old book. I've seen this flower."

"You've been to the Shrouded Sea?" Hannibal asked.

"I've seen visions," Zarah said. "I see it every night in my dreams. And I hear voices. For many years, the plants have talked to me. First the ones in our garden, then the trees, the fields. A few weeks ago, the World Flower broke through. It started sending me dreams and visions, and it told me to come find it. I know it holds the cure. I've felt its power. It's calling me, and I can guide you through the mists to find it."

She paused, and silence covered the deck. Alaric heard the waves sloshing against the hull of the ship. Distantly, a seagull called, and another answered. The crew sat, wide eyed and quiet, staring at Zarah.

"I know that sounds like madness," Alaric said. "But remember what you're really after: the treasure. Ten years of choice jewelry. No silver, no coins, only the richest gemstones. Every one of you could retire and live like a king. Every one of you. Isn't that worth the risk?"

The sailors started nodding along. Some closed their eyes, no doubt imagining what they would buy.

Hannibal shook his head. "You can't spend a copper farthing when you're dead, much less a king's ransom."

"If the treasure's even real," Rook said, "I know I'll die one day, but I'd rather not die chasing fairy tales."

Zarah pushed Alaric aside and stood before the crew. "Are you men or boys?"

"Say that again, and you'll find out," the boatswain said.

Hannibal laughed. "Calm down, Callum. She's a child herself. Let the girl speak."

"I thought you were sailors. Grown men and women. The crew of the great Scarlet Gray. I thought you were like your captain here," Zarah said. "You're scared of this? I'm a sixteen-year-old girl from a farm. I'm scared, but I'm doing this. And I will do this. I'll take a rowboat if I have to. What's wrong with you?"

Another murmur crossed the crew. They started looking at each other and talking back and forth.

"I don't like this," Alaric whispered. "The crew is balanced on a knife's edge."

"Then help me," Zarah said.

"Aye." Alaric stepped back to the front. "Zarah's a blunt farmgirl. She's got the manners of a goatherder, but she's got a point. This is the time to go big. If, you stay here, you risk nothing—and get nothing. No treasure, and no cure. If the plague hits, you die like anyone else."

"When the plague hits," Lamarca said. "Not if."

"Right. When the plague hits," Alaric said. "Yes, you might die if you go. But you'll die sailing, fighting, chasing glory. Not lying in bed drowning in your own snot. Come on! Lord Death is stalking all our shadows. Let him find us on our feet, chasing life!"

The crew went silent for a moment. The tension felt like a physical thing, a swelling wave that could break either way and sweep them all along. Alaric stood silent, trying to figure out how to make things break his way, but he couldn't find the words.

"Well said, Alaric of Port Theron," a deep voice rumbled. A pale, black-haired giant stepped forward. The first mate wore his long black hair shaved on the sides and pulled back in Solok warrior braids. Wearing them was an open challenge, an invitation to duel, any time, any place. Weak people didn't wear them for long.

The first mate was the first person Alaric had seen wearing a weapon aboard ship. A heavy, basket-hilted sword hung at his left hip. A buckler hung just behind it. On his right hip, he wore a knife so long it seemed like a second sword.

Alaric shuddered, but not from the sight of the blades. He saw weapons every day. They didn't scare him. The first mate's eyes scared him. His pale blue eyes stared coldly, bright with intelligence and suspicion. Alaric stood his ground. He refused to break the first mate's stare, even though he felt his chest tightening with fear. After a few moments, the big man smiled and nodded.

A tall Bosphori woman with skin like bronze stood to the first mate's left. Her sword looked lighter and faster than his, but just as deadly. Bosphori tended to be short, but she stood six feet tall.

She kept her black hair in the short braids common among her people. Traditional Bosphori patterns covered her black and yellow vest. Only master weavers could create that intricate angular knotwork. Her eyes swept across the newcomers with no less ferocity than the first mate's. The warrior woman's left eye was as dark as Alaric's, but her right was as blue as the midday sky. Alaric had never believed in omens, but he felt his disbelief begin to falter.

The captain chuckled. "Well, little brother, you do know how to make an entrance. Nikolos Mordos is my first mate, long-lost brother, able sailor, and unparalleled muscle. Second mate Damia Two-Eyes. I don't think I have to explain the nickname."

"Little?" Maxime whispered.

"Our guests are right," Nikolos said. "Lord Death comes for us all. We can defy him and fight for glory, or we can cower and live as his slaves. The sea wolves vote yes."

Damia nodded. "Aye, that we do."

Ten hard-eyed sailors gathered around Nikolos and Damia. "Aye! We vote aye!" They shouted together. "Go! Go! Go!"

The tension broke, and the mass of sailors joined their chant.

Callum and Hannibal shook their heads slowly. Rook Corbin shrugged.

"It looks like we have our answer," Captain Crimson said. "Ready the ship! We sail with the tide!"

Chapter 7

The sun was halfway up the eastern horizon, heating the wet salt air and signaling the change of tides. This was the best chance to leave the sheltered port and reach the open seas where the wind could fill their sails.

One of the Scarlet Gray's boats rowed the anchor out to the end of its chain, then dropped it. When it hit and set, six men turned the ship's great capstan wheel and took up the chain. The ship lurched toward its anchor and away from berth thirteen. When they reached the anchor, the sailors rowed it out again, then wheeled it in again.

Half the ships in port were moving out that morning. A good twenty stood ahead of them. Alaric watched as they rode into open water. He'd always been too busy to watch the ships get free. Port Theron was sheltered with a relatively narrow passage in and out, blocked partially by tall rock formations. The best ports offered not only a place to trade, but shelter from the hard sea winds.

The sailors moved with unity and purpose, like ten fingers on two hands. Alaric stood staring. He'd never seen such a thing. It wasn't the mechanical drill of marching soldiers, or the chaotic scrum of crowds. Every sailor knew their job, their role, and how to keep the ship moving. They hardly had to tell each other what to do. A few yells here, a few gestures there, the ship moved on.

The captain stood at the bow of the ship, tossing iron rings into the sea.

Alaric walked up to her. "I didn't take you for a religious woman."

"One more palm to grease, one more tax to pay," Jill said.

"It's a scam," Alaric said. "Any two-bit smith could make these rings—and charge almost nothing—but they only count if you buy them from the temple."

"Like I said, another tax to pay, another palm to grease." She tossed the last of the rings into the sea.

"Who knows if the Heavenly Lord of the Oceans exists?" Alaric said, "or if he even cares?"

"The Temple of the Sea exists, and the priests very much care about their tribute. It's an operating expense. I have enough enemies without making more by being cheap."

"Fair enough," Alaric said.

"Now run along. I've got things to do."

They sailed on through the morning, gliding across gentle seas. Alaric stood on the railing, watching his homeland diminish behind them. He'd always wanted to leave it behind. Now he was. It almost didn't seem real.

Once the ship hit open water, the crew relaxed back into individuals, milling about, waiting for a need to arise, then bursting into brief, furious action. Alaric felt the ship moving under his feet with the rhythm of the waves, an alien motion that only mildly upset him. He took a few tentative steps and quickly grew steady.

He found his way back to the professors. Maxime and Lamarca stood at the railing, pointing excitedly as a pod of dolphins broke the surface of the waves. Zarah stood beside them. She faced the same direction as the professors, but her gaze was a thousand miles away. Alaric glanced around the deck. The crew had begun to settle down.

"It's amazing how well the crew works together," Alaric said.

"Yes," Maxime said. "Like the fingers of one hand, or a healthy family."

"If you say so," Alaric said. "It's good for them, but not so good for us."

Zarah shook herself free from her thoughts and turned to look at him. "Did you say it was a bad thing? We need them to sail well. The Shrouded Sea won't be easy, even with the voices guiding us."

"Yes," Maxime said. "Why is that bad?"

"Because we're outside that family," Lamarca said. "That's what you're getting at, isn't it?"

"That's obvious," Zarah said. "Why are you worried about it now?"

"Open waters mean smooth sailing," Alaric said, "but what happens when things get dangerous?"

"They will get dangerous," Zarah said, "I doubt I'll return from the Shrouded Sea. I don't know about anyone else."

Alaric nodded. "We're going to need their help, but will we get it?"

"They'll fulfill their contract surely," Maxime said. "I think your time on the docks has made you overly suspicious. They'll do what they agree to."

"We may need them to do more than that," Lamarca said.

"We're here, but we're not really in. They still see us as passengers, outsiders, clients," Alaric said.

"We are outsiders," Zarah said.

Across the deck, a sailor dragged a bow across a cheap violin. Maxime winced at the poor quality of the sound, but Zarah smiled.

"That won't help us when we get to the island, when times get tough," Alaric said. "And the island will be dangerous, if that vision you showed me was real."

Zarah shivered. "It was real. It's all real."

"Then we need to build trust. They need to care about us by the time we get to the island," Alaric said. "I don't care what you think about them, but we can't be expendable."

"I'll talk to the fiddler," Zarah said. "I like this song anyway."

"I'll talk to the cook," Lamarca said. "I've always been interested in nautical applications of botanicals. I know it goes far beyond salted citrus and lime juice, but I'd love to see first-hand details."

Maxime looked around awkwardly. "I'll find something to do."

Zarah and Lamarca crossed the deck. The professor disappeared belowdecks. Zarah approached the fiddler, stepped into an open part of the deck, and started dancing. Alaric couldn't help but smile. She danced like a farmer, without elegance or pretense. She moved gracefully, like a workhorse finally set loose, racing across open fields. She spun around, and Alaric saw her smile. Genuine, wide, unguarded smiles were rare enough in Alaric's world. He'd never seen one from Zarah. She didn't trust or like him, and that made it hard to trust or like her. And she was either mad or touched by the divine, or both. But seeing her without the heavy weight of responsibility she carried, even for a moment, made him think again.

Zarah's dancing caught the crew's attention. One by one, the sailors came to join her. Soon, a circle dance had formed in the middle of the deck. Their feet beat in time against the deck like a circle of drums, until the sound almost drowned the fiddle. Another circle formed around, watching. Even the captain stopped to looked. She laughed and headed back to the bow. Then her brother stepped out from the deckhouse and waved.

"Nikolos?" Alaric whispered. "This could be important."

Alaric crept closer, the way he'd learned to do on the docks. It took him a long time to learn to look casual while sneaking, but it served him well. The only thing worse than being noticed was being obvious about trying not to be noticed. He pressed himself against the far side of the mast, vanishing in plain sight like he'd done so many times in Port Theron, and listened.

"We're going after Valens's jewels, Nikolos," the captain said. "What else do you want?"

"If we get this treasure? Nothing," Nikolos rumbled. "If the treasure is real, we'll have enough money to do whatever we want. I could take my share, pool it with a few men of mine, and buy a ship. Or bribe someone to look the other way while we steal one." The first mate frowned, looking down at his sister. "Come with me. Run up the black flag. Live free."

A chill ran across Alaric's shoulders, and his stomach clenched, but he forced himself to keep silent. The black flag meant piracy. Piracy meant violent lives and violent deaths. Fire and sword and grapeshot and the gallows when the navy caught them.

"We've had this conversation before, brother. My mind has not changed."

"I know your rules, all ten thousand of them. You pay more out in bribes then we would pay in powder for our cannons."

"There is no freedom living on the run from the navies of the Six Nations," Jill Crimson said. "There is no freedom in a body torn by grapeshot. No ship can ply the waves when its very sails have burned and its deck has been blasted to splinters. You think you can beat six navies? You think you can beat the great trade companies? By stealing a ship and going on a violent rampage? You'd be dead within a month's time."

"So, what?" Nikolos asked. "We choose no freedom or short-lived freedom?"

"I know the laws. I know the gaps in the laws. I can keep us sailing the gray forever. Who do we serve? No one. Who is hunting us?"

"No one," Nikolos said.

"And if this treasure is real, we alone stand to take it. Not the great merchant fleets, and not the pirates in Outlaw Cove. We will take it, the crew of the Scarlet Gray."

Mordos frowned, but the slight slump in his shoulders said he'd accepted defeat—for now. "You're the captain. We'll sail in the gray for now. But we will talk about this again, sister."

"Anytime you want, little brother."

Alaric held as still as a frightened mouse as Nikolos walked away. His heart pounded in his ears, and he didn't hear the captain's footsteps.

"I thought I smelled a wharf rat. Did you and Miss Remei plan this together, or did you just use her as a distraction?" She pointed at the circle of dancers.

"This was all me," Alaric said. "I promise. Zarah's just dancing."

The captain stared into his eyes. "So, the boy can tell the truth. Keep it up. Explain yourself."

Alaric looked up at the captain. "I was—"

"Eavesdropping," Jill said. "Don't waste your breath, boy. I've seen through much better liars than you."

Alaric spoke quickly, spinning his words as he went. "What if I was? I'm trusting my life to you. I'm trusting Zarah's life, and the professors' lives. I deserve to know what's going on. I deserve to know if you're going to run up the black flag and waylay a freighter instead of doing the job we hired you for. When I step foot on that island, I need to know who I can trust."

"When you step foot on that island?" The captain smiled. Her gold tooth caught a gleam of sunlight, but her look was as cold as a serpent's. "I never said you were going to the island."

"You made a promise. We had a deal. I get my share of the treasure. I come along on the ship. I—"

"I'll stand by the promises I made. But I never promised that you would step foot on the island." The captain's smile settled into a smirk, and Alaric hated her.

"I need to be there for Zarah and the professors."

"You want to be there for yourself," the captain said. "Don't lie to me, boy."

"You need me there. They trust me."

"I don't. If half the stories are true, this island will be lethal. There won't be room for a large shore party, and I've already got to carry that girl and those two robed professors. They're after the cure. They're my actual clients. You're just the dealmaker. Unless you prove that you will actually be valuable and not in the way, you're not going to be on my shore party. You understand, kid?"

"I am useful. I have skills, and not just at making deals. I made my own way on those docks. I'm a survivor."

The captain raised one eyebrow and smirked.

"I'm good with numbers. I remember everything I'm told. And I can do this." Alaric scrambled to the top of the wheelhouse. From there, he jumped to the yardarm and went hand over hand across. He dropped down near the railing, landing easily.

"Stop showing off, kid. You're going to break something," Jill said.

"I can take care of myself."

"I wasn't talking about your bones, boy. I was talking about my ship."

Alaric stared at her. "There's nothing I can do that is good enough for you, is there?"

"Not with an attitude like that. Either help or get out of the way. At least the scholars know how to be passengers."

Alaric stared at the captain, struck silent. A thousand things ran through his head to say, each one more useless than the one before. He wanted to curse and scream in anger. He thought of begging, of desperate attempts at logic and rhetoric. He could feel this opportunity slipping away. Even if they found Captain Valens's treasure, how could he trust they'd give his shares to him? And how could he prove his worth to the professors if he wasn't even there?

"I asked you a question, kid. You understand?"

"I heard you." Alaric's voice wavered but didn't break. "I heard you, Captain, but this isn't over."

"Whatever you say." The captain turned and walked away.

Chapter 8

Alaric stared out at the sea, his teeth grinding in frustration. Steel gray waves met a slate gray sky in the distance. He scanned the deck for a friendly face but saw only the backs of the sailors watching Zarah dance. Lamarca had not returned from her trip belowdecks to talk to the cook, and Maxime was nowhere in sight.

"Fine then, Captain Jill Crimson. If you want me to prove myself, I will." The ocean wind roared past his ears, carrying his words away. Alaric went looking for opportunity and found the boatswain.

"Mr. Westwind," Alaric said, "please allow me to introduce myself."

"You're the opportunistic little rat who's got us risking our lives for a fairy tale. And my name is Callum. I'm not a lord or merchant to be called mister."

"Callum," Alaric said, "think of the reward if we succeed. And you'll get an extra quarter share."

"One-and-a-quarter-shares of drowned and broken on the rocks of the Shrouded Sea?" Callum said with a rude snort. "You're with our clients, so I'll be civil, but don't try to win me over. I heard your speech like everyone else. I just didn't believe it."

"I know it's a big risk, but—"

"Just stop," the boatswain said. "We're doing this. The crew decided, and I'm a part of the crew. Stop trying to sell me on this foolishness. I don't believe it, and I don't think you believe it either. I think you have your own deal with the scholars, your own reasons to go to the Shrouded Sea. I think the treasure is just a tall tale you told to convince us to take you."

Alaric stepped back a bit. "That isn't true. The treasure might be real. We might find it."

Callum shook his head and laughed. "You half-believe it! You've almost started believing your own fairy tale. Oh, you're something. If I live to see the end of this, I'll have tales to tell, that's sure and certain. You just stay out of my way."

"Please," Alaric said, "let me ask one thing. One honest question. I'm not trying to sell you anything." He continued without giving the boatswain a chance to argue. "I overheard the first mate and the captain talking. He wants to take the ship into piracy."

Callum shrugged. "This isn't news, kid."

"The captain said no. Would he do it anyway?"

"He hasn't so far," Callum said.

"There's never been a treasure like this at stake," Alaric said.

"There still isn't," Callum said. "Nikolos is loyal to his sister. I know he's scary. But it's good to have someone scary on your side. Now get out of here. I have work to do."

Alaric left Callum and went to find the quartermaster, Hannibal Three-Fingers.

"Alaric of Port Theron!" Hannibal greeted him with a wide, bright smile.

Alaric smiled back. "I'm glad to see you. I know you were skeptical about this journey, and I wanted to make sure we were all right."

The quartermaster laughed. "Oh, I've made peace with this whole mad mission. When we run short of food, we'll throw you overboard first."

"I appreciate the loyalty," Alaric said.

"You're lucky Kartargans are civilized," Hannibal said. "A Solokhoi would cut you up and use your parts for fish bait." He grinned like death. "The first mate is Solok, isn't he?"

"That's specific," Alaric said.

"It's the only thing a slimy little opportunist like yourself is good for. Even Solok aren't cannibals." The quartermaster shuddered at the thought. "You hear stories at sea, but I'd sooner drown myself."

"Speaking of Solokhoi," Alaric said, "the first mate wants to take the ship into piracy, but the captain says no. Would he do it anyway?"

Hannibal laughed. "Only a passenger would ask such a foolish question. Nikolos Mordos? Betray his own sister? Have you been drinking seawater?"

"He met us armed. He's not like the rest of the crew," Alaric said.

"We all know he wants to be a pirate. So what? Half the crew would go with him. I know I would," the quartermaster said, "and we all know he won't do it without his sister. He doesn't want to be captain. He wants to rule the seas with her."

"You're sure of that?" Alaric said.

"Yeah. I'm sure. And I'll do it. I'll follow Jill Crimson whether she's sailing the gray or running up the black flag." Hannibal grinned. "I'm following her into this death trap."

"Do you always sound this happy?" Alaric asked.

"My demeanor is my choice." Hannibal held up his hand. "When I lost these two fingers, I had a choice. I could resent the world for my loss, or I could keep smiling and fighting. I chose the latter. And I'm going to do the same thing on this trip, until you get us all killed."

Heat rose in Alaric's cheeks as the quartermaster spoke. "I'm beginning to grasp the depths of your disrespect for me," he said. "But you're wrong. You think I'm just a worthless dealmaker? You think I only spin the truth and scam tourists?"

"If the shoe fits."

"I've made my living by my wits since I was a child. I learned to outwit, outrun, and outmaneuver people twice my age and three times my size. I not only survived by myself, but I earned a reputation. I'm the best messenger on the docks. Ask anyone in Port Theron. Important people trust me to get the job done."

"We're far from your docks, boy," Hannibal said. "That's worthless out here."

"My speed, my agility, my intelligence, my instincts, and my determination are not worthless. They matter wherever I am. Don't tell me that."

"We saw your instincts this morning. They're sharp, but self-serving. They won't help the rest of us. Just don't get in our way."

"I'm not going to earn your respect, am I?" Alaric asked.

Hannibal laughed a big, booming laugh. "The omens and the four winds all say no."

Alaric walked away with the quartermaster's laugh echoing behind him. "Fine. If I can't win Collum and Hannibal over, I'll make them irrelevant, like I did at the meeting." He wandered across the deck, listening to bits and pieces of the crew's conversations, looking for opportunities.

He found one quickly: a group of sailors talking loudly about treasure.

Alaric hurried over. "What's the news?"

"Hey! You're with the passengers. Alaric, right?" a wiry man with wild black hair said. "I'm Gorvin. You good with numbers?"

"Absolutely," Alaric said. "What's the question?"

"We're trying to figure out how much treasure we'll each get," a thin sailor said. "You know what I mean?"

"That's Behir," Gorvin said. The thin sailor nodded in introduction. "The blonde man's Lirrin."

"Good to meet you," Lirrin said.

Alaric licked his lips, as he often did when he was figuring numbers. "Each sailor gets a share. The captain gets two. The first mate gets one and a half. The boatswain and quartermaster get one and a quarter each. The number of shares equals the number of people on the boat, plus two. Am I right?"

"Yeah, kid. You got it," Lirrin said.

"Just so you know," Alaric said, "we're taking two shares between the four of us for bringing you to the treasure."

"Sounds fair enough. Just two shares, and there's four of you."

"Right." Alaric didn't mention that he was getting both of those extra shares. "So that gives us a number of shares equal to the number of sailors plus four. One for the captain, one for the other officers, and two for us. You follow?"

The sailors nodded along.

"Your crew has forty-four sailors, right? Not counting the captain, first mate, boatswain, and quartermaster?" Alaric asked.

"How did you know?" Gorvin asked.

"Back in Port Theron, the captain said she'd have to divide the treasure fifty ways," Alaric said. "She either meant fifty shares or fifty sailors. She seems like a precise person, so I assume she meant fifty shares. So, that gives us fifty-two shares for this job."

"Right," Gorvin said. "Let's say we get a thousand gold coins. That's a lot, right?"

"That's not what I'd call a legendary treasure," Alaric said. "Remember the story?"

"Right! Right!" Behir said. "Captain Valens stole the choicest gems and jewelry from his own crew for ten years."

"He took them off the top of each job," Lirrin said.

"I heard he even killed some of his own crew when they found out," Gorvin added.

"Woo," Behir said, "there's no telling how big that haul might be."

Alaric smiled. "It might be ten thousand gold draca. If so, you'd end up with one hundred and ninety-two each, plus some silver."

The three sailors whistled low.

"I could retire on half that," Behir said, "and live better than I've ever lived."

"If the stories are true, Valens's treasure could be worth much more than ten thousand," Alaric said.

"I can't even imagine that much money," Gorvin said. "I've never even seen a gold draca. It's like a year's wages for a skilled craftsman, all in one coin!"

"It's hard to imagine," Lirrin said. "We don't often have passengers who can do math. Not like the captain and the quartermaster. Especially not a kid like you. No disrespect."

"I have a good mind for numbers," Alaric said. "I had to learn how to count my own change. I've been on my own since I was a little boy. When you're a kid, you learn to watch your back. Everybody on that dock tried to get one over on me." He scowled. "I taught them not to, in time."

"Well, I don't see how anyone could try that now," Lirrin said.

"Yes, yes, you're very smart." Captain Jill Crimson's voice startled the three sailors. They jolted like they'd been caught doing something wrong. "As you were, men. We're still in smooth waters. But keep your wits about you and try not to spend too much time dreaming of gold."

"Yes, Captain!" the sailors said.

She nodded curtly, and the sailors scattered. "You're good at math. So is my quartermaster. So's Rook Corbin. You wouldn't know it to look at him, but he's a smart man. I get the feeling you're smart too." She frowned. "But not, perhaps, as smart as you think. And not smarter than I am."

"What do you mean?" Alaric said. "I was just making conversation, helping them answer a question."

"Stop lying to me, boy," the captain said. "You were filling their heads with visions of gold and treasure. You started at ten times their number and worked your way up from there."

"They were thinking too small," Alaric said. "If this treasure's real, it's really big."

"If I'd been a minute later, you'd have had those fools counting on a million gold draca. Maybe a million each."

"That much would be ridiculous," Alaric said, "even for a legend."

Jill chuckled. "I'll motivate my crew. I don't need you manipulating them."

Alaric looked up at the captain. "I'm not trying to undermine you as captain. That's the last thing I need. I need this to work. I need that treasure. I need to never have to go back to that hand-to-mouth, dock-rat existence again. So, I will keep talking to your sailors. And I will answer questions when I am asked. And I will learn what I can learn from them and teach them what I can teach them."

"Will you?" Jill asked.

Alaric felt his face burning, felt cold sweat on the edges of his hairline. He knew deep down he was not the captain's equal. He was pretty sure she knew that, too, and that meant it was even more vital that he not admit it. "I need them to trust me, like me, and respect me. I need to prove my worth, so I can get to that island."

"You won't get there by playing my men for greedy fools. Bye, kid." Jill walked away with a dismissive little wave.

"Maybe not," Alaric said, "but I will get there. Watch me." He saw Rook Corbin at the wheel and headed toward him. "Hi, Rook!"

"Callum and Hannibal still sore at you?" Rook asked.

"You saw?" Alaric said.

"If we find the treasure, they'll come around," Rook said. "They'll probably forget they ever doubted you."

"What about you?" Alaric asked. "Are we good? You didn't want to come either."

"I go where the Scarlet Gray goes," Rook said. "I'm not mad."

"You're not worried we'll all starve?" Alaric said.

"No, we won't starve," Rook said. "We'll smash against the rocks and sink long before we run out of food." Rook laughed. "I'm not mad."

"You're not? You just said you thought we were going to die."

"We all have to die sometime. I doubt this treasure is real, but we're sailing. We're taking a chance. We're in this together, so I'm going to be in. That's the only way I know how to live. Callum and Hannibal would be a lot happier if they got that."

"That's philosophical," Alaric said. "Enlightened even."

The old sailor laughed. "Rook Corbin, guru of wisdom and enlightenment. Who'd have thought it?"

"Rook, can I ask you for help?" Alaric asked.

"You can always ask."

"I need two things, really," Alaric said. "Information and help. I heard Nikolos and the captain talking about going pirate."

"She didn't change her answer, did she?"

"No. Do they have that conversation often?"

The old sailor shook his head. "Every time we put out to sea."

"Would Nikolos ever move without the captain?" Alaric asked. "Would he ever move against her?"

Rook ran his hand through his graying hair. "That's the kind of question that starts trouble."

"The boatswain and the quartermaster trust him completely," Alaric said. "Hannibal says he'd gladly follow him."

"They would," Rook said. "They would."

"But you won't?"

"Everyone says Nikolos loves his sister and will follow her anywhere." Rook paused. "And maybe he does."

"But?" Alaric asked.

"They forget that Nikolos and the captain didn't grow up together. I've known Captain Crimson longer than he has. I don't want to start any trouble. I haven't seen anything new or specific, but I don't know. He's big, he's proud, he's mean, and he's always armed. He keeps saying he wants us all to go pirate. I've never been an officer. I've never been a great leader or wise man. But when somebody goes to that much trouble to show who he is, I tend to believe him."

Rook's words settled like a weight in Alaric's stomach. "I didn't want to hear that."

"I reckon you didn't."

"Is it strange that I'm relieved?" Alaric asked.

"Relieved?"

"I don't want to be the only one aboard who doesn't trust him."

Rook shrugged. "It will probably come to nothing. What else did you need?"

"Captain Crimson said I won't be on the shore party unless I prove myself valuable and trustworthy. I don't know how to earn her respect, but I have to go to that island. I have to help Zarah find the World Flower. I'm trying to get into the university, and those scholars are my ticket. They're here for Zarah, and so I need to be there for them all."

"I can't change the captain's mind, if that's what you're asking," Rook said.

"No, but you can teach me how to sail," Alaric said. "Maybe if I show her that I can learn and take instruction, she'll see I'm worth taking along."

Rook shrugged. "Worth a shot, I guess. Here. Let me show you how to steer. When my turn at the wheel's up, I can show you knotwork."

"Thank you," Alaric said. "I won't forget this."

He watched Rook steer for almost an hour, memorizing every word of direction the sailor gave.

"We're in open water," Rook said. "There's nothing here to hit. You take a turn." Rook stepped back, and Alaric took the wheel.

"It wants to move on its own!" Alaric said.

"Just a little," Rook said. "The ship is connected to the rudder with pulleys. You're feeling the force of the ocean. The sea's calm enough now. You should see it in a storm. One night, the seas got so rough Nikolos and Hannibal had to steer together. It took both of them to keep us on course. Seeing those two big men fighting the wheel…. That's a sight I won't forget."

Alaric nodded. He could feel the wheel wavering in his hands, feel the whole ship beneath his feet. "You turn the wheel the direct you want to go, or the opposite?"

"You don't turn the wheel at all," Captain Crimson said from behind him.

Alaric jolted, but he kept his hands on the wheel.

"Rook, what are you thinking, letting this boy steer my ship?"

"All due respect, Captain, I was younger than Alaric the first time I had my hands on a wheel," Rook said. "It's calm seas, and I spent the last hour teaching him what to do."

"Then you wasted your hour," Jill said. "Alaric, I know what you're trying to do, but distracting my crew isn't going to get you to the island."

"What will?" Alaric asked.

"It's not my job to figure that out for you, kid. Now get your hands off my wheel." The captain walked away with another infuriating little wave.

Alaric sank back against the wall of the wheelhouse. "I know what I have to do."

"What's that?" Rook asked.

"There's only one person who can help me now, the one person I don't want to ask for help." Alaric looked across the deck and saw Nikolos Mordos with his hand on the hilt of his sword.

"Him?" Rook laughed. "Good luck, kid. You're going to need it."

Chapter 9

A warm breeze blew across the ocean, but anger formed like ice in Alaric's gut. He walked to the rail where Zarah and the professors stood watching the sea.

"The dancing did me good." Zarah stretched and smiled. "The noise of the earth and the plants is quiet, but the World Flower is calling even louder. We're sailing right. Do you think we'll see more dolphins?"

"There is an excellent chance." Maxime gestured with one hand while holding tightly to the railing with the other. "They seem to be quite common here, although we are moving farther into the open ocean. As I recall, prey fish are scarcer here, and so one would expect fewer larger animals. Hi, Alaric. I see you've been mingling with the crew a bit more than we have."

"Speak for yourself," Lamarca said. "I had a fascinating chat with the cook."

"I'm not on the shore crew." Alaric dropped the phrase into the conversation like a stone into a small pool.

"What?" Maxime asked. "You're one of us. We need you there."

"You've only known him a day longer than you've known them," Zarah said.

"They've known each other for years. They don't care about us," Lamarca said.

"You're on the shore party because you have to be," Alaric said. "She thinks I'm just the dealmaker. I'm not giving up."

"I saw what you did on that yardarm," Lamarca said. "The captain was right. It was dangerous. And she doesn't need you on the shore party. You might be a liability to her."

"I will not—"

"Let me finish," Professor Lamarca said. "She doesn't need you, but we need you. We know what you can do. We know how you act under pressure. But she doesn't know any of that. All she knows is that you're showing off, you're making deals, and you're getting in her way."

"What?" Maxime asked.

"You don't understand what it's like to be a woman in authority," Lamarca said. "Everybody questions you. Everybody challenges you. You have to work twice as hard as a man if you want any respect, and you can't let anything get past you."

Maxime raised his eyebrows. "I was not aware."

"And that's just at the university," Lamarca said. "Captain Crimson deals in life and death matters."

"So what?" Alaric said. "I'm not going to respect her authority if it keeps me off that island. This is a once in a lifetime chance for me. This can change everything. I'm not giving up."

Professor Lamarca shrugged. "You do what you have to do. I just wanted to let you know what she's seeing."

"You've talked to everyone but the cook," Zarah said. "Who's left?"

Alaric pointed across the deck. "Him."

Nikolos Mordos stood at the prow, staring at the sea, his hand resting on the hilt of his sword.

"The first mate?" Maxime asked. "Why? He's dangerous, he takes what he wants, and he knows how to manipulate the crew. Why would you want—oh, that's exactly why you want him to help you."

Alaric smiled grimly. "Now you're getting it." He felt Zarah's hand heavy on his shoulder.

"Be careful," she said. "I don't trust him."

"Trust has nothing to do with it."

Alaric stared up at the first mate. Nikolos Mordos stood more than a foot taller than Alaric and had the lean, wiry muscles of a killer.

"Out with it, boy," Nikolos said. "I'm not a passenger. I have things to do."

"Will you teach me to fight?" Alaric asked.

The first mate laughed. "Why?"

"I never had a chance to learn," Alaric said.

"That's not my problem."

"I never had anyone to teach me how to fight. It's not the kind of thing you can learn by yourself," Alaric said. "I learned to run, to climb, to jump, to hide, to play dirty, to creep through places others wouldn't or couldn't. When you're a kid working the streets with no one to protect you, you learn or you die." Alaric felt his throat tightening. He was telling Mordos a lot. He hoped it would be worth it.

Nikolos frowned. "I grew up without family. My mother did what she had to do to survive and keep me alive. We had no one else. I learned to fight the hard way." The big man's face showed the scars those lessons had left. "All right. Go below and fetch two wasters. Wooden swords. I'll train you. You'll obey me, or you'll regret it."

"Thank you," Alaric said.

"Don't thank me yet," Nikolos said with a wolf's grin.

"Why are you helping me?" Alaric asked. "No one else trusts me."

Nikolos laughed. "You're hungry. You want this. You need this. I can work with hunger. Now fetch the swords, boy. I can work with hunger. I can't abide hesitation or sloth."

Alaric spent the first day learning how to stand and hold the sword. He practiced the most basic cuts and parries until his arms burned.

"It hurts?" Nikolos asked. "Good. Keep practicing!"

Alaric kept on until his arms went numb and his hands grew cold and trembling. He stopped to rub the feeling back into his fingers.

"Giving up already?" Nikolos asked.

"No." Alaric's fingers burned and stung as he flexed them. "I think I'm getting it."

"Show me."

Alaric swung the wooden blade, just as he'd been shown.

"No." Nikolos slapped the flat of Alaric's sword with his own. "Your edge alignment's off. You cut with the edge, not the flat part."

"I was cutting with the edge," Alaric said.

"You think you know how to fight now?" The first mate's voice darkened. "You want to try sparring?"

Alaric's face went cold at the thought, but he gritted his teeth and did not back down.

Nikolos laughed. "You've got spirit, but you're not ready for that. Wait here." He returned with a scrap of thick rope and a cutlass. He hung the rope from a crossbeam and handed Alaric the sword.

"I say your edge alignment is bilge. You say you're cutting with the edge. Prove it."

Alaric cut at the rope. His sword bit in a little, but the rope swung out of the way, mostly uncut. He looked down at his sword. It looked sharp.

"Again," Nikolos said. "The blade is sharp. You're the dull one. Do it again."

Alaric tried again, from a different angle. This time, he cut into the rope about a quarter of an inch before it swung free. He tried again and again, but never got more than a quarter inch into the rope.

"It can't be done," Alaric said.

Nikolos took the sword from his hands and cut the rope in one stroke.

Alaric's face turned red. Shame rose inside him like a chattering crowd, calling him worthless, telling him he'd never be more than he is. He'd failed to prove himself. He'd failed. He stood there, stunned and silent.

Fortunately, Nikolos couldn't hear the crowd. He pressed the wooden sword back into Alaric's hand. "Your edge alignment won't fix itself. Get back to work."

Alaric spent the rest of the day practicing the same beginner's cuts.

"Your form is still terrible," Nikolos said, "but it's less terrible than it was this morning. You can come back tomorrow if you still want to learn."

The next morning broke ugly. Low gray clouds filled the sky, blocking the sunrise. The eastern horizon held no gold or orange, just a slightly lighter gray.

"You've looked better," Zarah said as Alaric stumbled onto deck. "You almost missed breakfast."

"Ugh," Alaric grumbled.

"You look as gray as the morning." Maxime pressed a cup of something hot and sour into his hands.

Alaric struggled to keep hold of the cup.

"Lime juice and hot grog," Professor Lamarca said. "It's not coffee, but it keeps scurvy at bay."

"I'm guessing you trained a bit too hard with our Solok friend," Maxime said.

Alaric groaned. "I hurt in places I've never hurt before."

"Did you at least learn a lot?"

"I practiced five cuts and five parries," Alaric said. "Nikolos said my form is terrible. I don't know what I'm even doing there. He's making me look like a fool."

"Have you ever trained with a sword before?" Maxime asked.

"When would I have learned?" Alaric asked. "I know how to stab with a knife. I know how to punch and kick and bite and get free if someone grabs me. But I learned all that the hard way. The Thervingi Royal Dueling Society's dues were out of my budget."

"Fair enough," Maxime said.

"I don't know what I'm doing. I'll never prove myself to the captain this way. I'm wasting my time."

"You just said you're a beginner," Zarah said. "Why wouldn't you want to start with the basics? You don't know anything."

"I feel like a fool. I'm no good at this."

"If you were good at it, you wouldn't need a teacher," Zarah said. "What's wrong with you? Eat your porridge and go to your lesson!"

"Fine," Alaric said, "I'll go."

The next two days went much like the first. Every day, Alaric struggled and failed, but every day his form got better. On the third day, Nikolos hung the rope again, and Alaric cut it.

"Good! You've learned to cut," Nikolos said. "Come back tomorrow, and I'll teach you to parry."

Alaric woke with the sun's first rays. He ate a hot bowl of porridge and watched the sunrise paint the horizon gold and orange. Then, he hurried to find the first mate.

Nikolos stood waiting for him with two swords formed from semi-flexible bamboo strips.

"These are different," Alaric said.

"Your edge alignment is good enough for now," Nikolos said. "Today you'll be practicing defense."

"Why bamboo?" Alaric asked.

"Because I'd split your skull if I hit you with a wooden sword," Nikolos said.

"Why do I have a bamboo sword?" Alaric said.

"Because I'd split your skull if you hit me with a wooden sword."

"Oh." Alaric's throat tightened at the thought.

Nikolos grinned. "Don't let me get into your head, boy. Begin!"

Nikolos swung his sword down. Alaric swept his up and blocked it. The bamboo swords smacked together with a loud crack. Nikolos swept his sword in a downward arc, and pain exploded through Alaric's leg.

Nikolos laughed. "It hurts?"

"Yes."

"Then don't get hit." Nikolos swung a hard strike from the right.

Alaric raised his sword to block it. A shock went through his arm as the blades collided. He swung left just in time to catch the big man's follow-up. "I'm getting it!"

Nikolos laughed and attacked again. Alaric blocked low. The bamboo blades met with a smack.

"I'm getting this!" Alaric laughed as he blocked another strike.

Nikolos chuckled. He attacked again, faster this time.

Alaric barely blocked it. The second attack came flashing in. Alaric jumped back, and it missed him by inches.

"Not bad, boy." Nikolos pressed the attack, pushing Alaric back. Again and again, the bamboo blades clacked together. Alaric kept retreating, barely blocking each strike, until he hit the wheelhouse wall and could retreat no further.

Then pain burst through his left arm.

Another hard strike stung Alaric's leg. He blocked a third strike, but the follow-up knocked the sword from his hand.

Alaric stared up at Nikolos. The big man's blue eyes gleamed.

"Nikolos?" Alaric said quietly.

"Heh." The first mate stepped back. "Pretty good for a kid. But you have to learn to stand your ground. You won't always be able to run away."

Alaric nodded. "Yes, sir."

"Don't call me sir. I'm not the captain," Nikolos said. "Now pick that sword up. Your lesson isn't over."

Alaric's hand trembled as he reached for the bamboo sword. He felt welts rising on his skin, deepening into bruises.

He stood anyway, holding the sword in front of him. His hands shook, setting the bamboo blade wobbling. But he met the first mate's gaze. "Let's do this."

"You are hungry," Nikolos said. "Good. That's enough for today. Your body can only take so much. Get some sleep. Tomorrow will be a hard day."

Day after day, Alaric fought through sore muscles and bruised limbs. Every part of him hurt, even the parts Nikolos hadn't hit. After another week, he could block most of Nikolos's attacks, even with the first mate's massive reach advantage. He could return an attack, quickly striking back from a block. He even grazed Nikolos's wrist, though not hard enough for the big man to notice.

"I think that one almost hit me, boy. Good." Nikolos laughed. "Look at you. Ten days and you're already better than Rook Corbin!"

Alaric grinned, feeling a burst of pride welling up inside him. He raised the bamboo sword above his head and laughed out loud. "Thank you! Thank you. I mean it."

"Glad to do it, Alaric. We might make a swordsman out of you yet. That's enough for today, kid. See you tomorrow."

Alaric barely felt his feet touching the deck as he put away the bamboo swords. When he emerged from below, he saw Zarah with the scholars and hurried over. "Did you see that? Nikolos Mordos said I was already better than Rook Corbin."

"I think everybody on board ship saw and heard that." Zarah wrinkled her nose and grinned. "Especially the victory cry at the end."

"It was a good showing," Maxime said, "against a fearsome foe. One can hardly blame the young man for celebrating."

"And he called me Alaric! Not boy or kid, but Alaric!"

"Congratulations," Zarah said.

Alaric looked at her.

"I mean it," she said. "I'm not the one who lies. You earned this the hard way. No tricks, no shortcuts. Good job."

Alaric smiled. "That means something from you."

Zarah shrugged and blushed a little. "Don't get used to it."

Alaric's smile turned calculating. "With that kind of praise for the first mate, the captain will have to let me on the shore party. This surely has to be enough to prove to her—"

"Hey, kid, you'll learn a lot more if you actually focus on learning something instead of proving yourself." Alaric turned around and saw the captain there, that same terrible smirk on her face.

"Surely this is enough!" Alaric said.

"You'll never beat my brother anyway. No one on this ship can. He's going easy on you because you're a kid."

"He said—"

"If he wanted to, he could have that sword out of your hands in a second," Jill said. "I've seen him do it to professional soldiers and mercenaries."

"Is that what it would take to prove myself?" Alaric asked. "Being the best swordsman on the ship?"

"You keep trying to show off, to impress me. I'm a grown woman, kid. I've seen it all. It won't work."

"What do I have to do to convince you?" Alaric asked.

Jill gave no answer. She only turned and walked away.

"Captain!" Alaric shouted. "You and me!"

She stopped and half-turned. "Are you challenging me, boy? Without a full fortnight of training behind you?"

"Bamboo swords. Tomorrow at dawn."

The captain burst out laughing. "Go get your little toy swords. I don't have time for this. I'm going to shut you up right now."

Alaric hurried belowdecks to get the bamboo swords and almost ran into Nikolos.

The first mate shook his head and chuckled a deep, rumbling laugh. "You really are hungry."

"Any advice?"

"Don't try to hit her in the face. She might show mercy if you don't." Nikolos scowled, then grinned. "Go on. Make your mistake. If you're going to be a fool, be a bold one."

By the time Alaric got the swords and returned to the deck, a circle of sailors had formed around the captain. He recognized Rook Corbin, Gorvin, Behir, and Lirrin. He saw the red of Collum Westwind's hair and heard Hannibal's distinctive laugh. Nikolos and Damia stood back, watching silently.

"Captain," Alaric said, "I'm ready."

Gorvin stepped up and took the swords. The wild-haired sailor didn't even look at Alaric. He checked over both of them quickly, then offered them to the captain. She tossed one to Alaric and kept one for herself.

Alaric caught the sword by the bamboo blade and shifted his grip.

"Ready?" Gorvin asked. "Begin!" He scrambled out of their way.

The captain circled closer. The tip of her sword dipped just a bit, but Alaric didn't take the bait. She swung lightly, from the wrist, slapping her sword against his. He overcorrected, and she slashed high.

Alaric blocked like Nikolos had shown him, and the bamboo blades cracked together.

"Not bad, kid." Jill swung the sword around, striking at his left shoulder. Alaric stepped back and parried, just stopping the blow.

Jill circled her blade around to threaten his arm. Alaric slid back and pulled his arm in, and her strike fell short. Alaric could feel the bodies of the sailors behind him. He didn't have far to go.

"I know my brother didn't teach you to retreat."

"No, he didn't!" Alaric lunged toward the captain, point first.

Captain Crimson sidestepped and knocked the sword just out of line. Alaric's momentum carried him forward and put him off-balance for just a second.

But a second was all it took. The captain swept her sword down onto Alaric's hand, hard.

"Augh!" Alaric's sword clattered to the ground.

Jill wasn't done. Her bamboo blade slapped him hard on the bicep, then on his back. "Do I need to continue?"

Alaric staggered in pain and surprise. He held his hand while his vision returned to normal.

"I didn't think so." Jill tossed her sword at Alaric's feet. "Now get out of my sight."

Alaric staggered belowdecks to nurse his pain in the darkened hold. Belowdecks smelled of salt, tar, gunpowder, and old onions. He crawled into a corner, sat on a roughly woven cargo net, and hid. He felt wetness on his face but refused to acknowledge tears. There was no room on this ship for tears, any more than there was room on the docks of Port Theron.

He sat in the dark, in silence, until a voice broke through. One of the last voices he wanted to hear right now.

"I think I found him!" Zarah called. "Hey, you're good at hiding."

"Go away." Alaric tried to wipe his face with his other hand, but it was still a mess.

"Let me look at that hand," Zarah said.

"You a healer?"

"Suit yourself," Zarah said.

"No. Don't go." Alaric offered up his right hand.

Zarah's hands were strong and bigger than Alaric's, but they were warm and gentle. "It's not broken. You're lucky. She didn't hit you that hard."

"Hard enough." Alaric stared up at her.

"Did she hit you in the head?" Zarah asked. "You're staring."

Lamarca kneeled down next to them. "Sometimes a sharp hit can cause the hand to open or go limp for a second."

Maxime joined them a moment later. "Nothing permanently damaged? Good."

"What am I going to do?" Alaric hung his head. "I need to be a part of this. I deserve to be a part of this. It was part of our deal. I was coming along for the whole thing."

Professor Lamarca held up her hand to stop Maxime from talking. "I'm no expert on sailors or pirates, but I am a woman with authority. And I often have to deal with men undermining that authority. I also have to accept unqualified and uncommitted men as equals."

"I'm not—" Alaric said.

"Don't interrupt me," Lamarca said. "I've had to deal with men feeling entitled to a voice, even a controlling voice, in everything I do. I understand where she's coming from."

"Then what do I do? How do I prove to her that I'm not just a passenger? I'm not some dealmaker who stays on shore and leaves the danger to someone else. I'm a part of this now. I'm all in." He shook his head. "But it doesn't matter! I've tried everything!"

"No, you haven't tried everything," Zarah said. "You haven't asked for help."

"I thought you didn't trust me. You said I was only in this for myself."

"I still don't trust you much," Zarah said, "but I trust you more than I trust Nikolos or Damia."

"And I trust you," Lamarca said. "Let us talk to the captain. Trust us for once."

"Thank you," Alaric said.

Zarah and Lamarca came back a few minutes later.

"The captain wants to speak to you," Lamarca said.

"What should I say?" Alaric asked.

"Tell her how committed you are to seeing this through."

"Stop showing off," Zarah added. "Stop trying to prove yourself, and just tell her."

"Just tell her?" The rage and frustration in Alaric's chest bubbled down to a cold fear. "Just tell her? Tell her I expect her to honor her promise, and that I am prepared to honor mine, and then…what? Just accept her response?"

"I know you don't want to hear this," Lamarca said, "but this is her ship. So yes, respect her answer."

They went up the stairs together. Ahead, Captain Crimson crossed the deck at a sharp, fast walk. As she moved, she checked the sails, the ship, and the crew. "You're right, Professor Lamarca. This is her ship. I'll do it."

Alaric took a deep breath and walked across the deck, trying to match the captain's confidence. The ship moved beneath his feet, or maybe his nerves made him unsteady.

"Captain Crimson, I need to speak with you."

She kept watching the sea. "I can hear you."

"When I brought you this opportunity, when I told you about the treasure, we made a deal." Alaric's mouth went dry. He hoped his voice wouldn't crack mid-sentence. "I am committed to that deal. I'm not a passenger. I'm not a dealmaker who stays ashore. I'm in this to the end."

She closed the telescope and turned to look at him. "I need to know you will not be a liability."

"I'm long past trying to prove myself to you. Nothing I can do on this ship will be enough. I'm only making myself a fool by trying. For that, I'm sorry."

Jill chuckled. "I guess every court needs a jester."

"I've come to care about Zarah and the professors," Alaric said. "I don't want them to be on that island without someone who's really on their side. Zarah, Professor Lamarca, and Professor Maxime want me there. They need me there. So, I need to be on that boat."

The captain raised one eyebrow but said nothing.

"But I understand that this is your ship, and I will abide by your decision."

Jill stared at him for a long time, her dark eyes reading his. "That's the first thing you've said to me that wasn't wrapped in grease and spun sugar." She clapped him on the shoulder, right where she'd hit him earlier. Alaric winced, and the captain laughed. "Good man. Keep your gear ready and your eyes open."

"Really?" Alaric asked. "You're letting me go to the island?"

"I'm promising you a chance to prove yourself," the captain said, "I'm promising you a chance to earn your spot on the shore party. Keep your nose clean and pay attention. You won't get many chances." Jill grinned. "You didn't think that would work, did you?"

"Honestly, no," Alaric said. "Thank you, Captain. I won't forget this."

"Don't thank me yet. You're not there yet." The captain looked to the east. "We'll be making a hard turn soon. The Shrouded Sea is near. I can smell it. Let's hope your friend can get us through the mists, or none of us will reach the island."

Chapter 10

As the Scarlet Gray sailed south across calm and empty seas, Alaric's pride and body healed. His right hand swelled and throbbed. His bruises passed through purple into green, and then yellow, before finally vanishing into the same bronze as the surrounding skin.

Three days after his foolhardy duel with the captain, the ship turned hard to port.

"They're turning east. Good." Zarah stared across the empty water. "We'll enter the Shrouded Sea from the west. That will be better sailing. Safer. Not safe." She shuddered.

Alaric pointed to a bird soaring in the western sky. "That's the first bird I've seen all week. I think it's an albatross."

"They know the Shrouded Sea is not theirs," Zarah said.

"What?" Alaric asked. "They? Who?"

"The birds. The fish. The creatures of this world."

"Who…or what…does it belong to?" Alaric asked.

"The World Flower." Zarah tensed like she was expecting a fight. "And whatever can grow in its shadow, pure or wicked."

Alaric saw fear in her green eyes. The vison rushed back, half memory, half nightmare. As strong as when he'd first seen it in the Port Theron coffee shop. Twisted men of vine and thorn, hungry for blood, calling her name.

"We're with you," Alaric said. "Don't worry."

Zarah's shoulders relaxed, and her fists unclenched. "Thanks. It means a lot to not be alone." She looked to the east. Already the horizon had grown indistinct, misty. "We're almost there."

"Are you ready?"

Zarah gazed at the white haze on the horizon. "I am, and I'm not. I know the voice will guide me through."

"You don't sound relieved."

She shuddered. "The voice started out as just a voice. It rose above the background noise of plants and the earth. But the closer we get to the island, the stronger it gets."

"You can guide us through, right?" Alaric said.

"The voice will guide us through. I'm not sure how much of me will be there. I'm not sure how much of me will be left when this is over."

Alaric reached up and touched Zarah's shoulder. "I'll be here for whatever's left of you."

She smiled. "Thanks."

At dawn, the Scarlet Gray faced the Shrouded Sea. A wall of gray-white mist rose from the surface of the ocean. It reached far into the blurry heights of the sky.

"The fog!" Rook called out. "We've reached the Shrouded Sea!"

Alaric looked ahead. "That's not a shroud. It's a wall."

The cool breath of fog overwhelmed the salt of the sea and the wood and tar of the ship. The world ahead lay silent and utterly, deathly still.

"Miss Remei, it's time," Jill said. The captain strode to the front of the ship, and Zarah followed.

The sailors crowded around. They stared into the wall of mist, squinting to see through.

"Captain, I hope she can navigate through that," Rook said, "because we can't. We can't see where we're going. I can't see a thing."

"You don't have to," Zarah said.

"We know there are rocks out there," Callum said. "We know ships go in and never return. Are you sure you want to do this?"

"Can we even sail through that?" Gorvin asked.

"Yeah, how do we steer?" Behir said.

"I can guide us through," Zarah said. "The voice will guide me."

"Oh, we are all going to die," Callum said.

Hannibal laughed. "At least we won't starve."

"Silence!" Captain Crimson turned on her crew with the rage of the sea in her eyes. "You had your say when we took this job. You know the rules. We decide together, and then we're in, together. All in! You don't get to change your minds now. You had your say, and now you'll do your part." She stared from one sailor to another. No one held her gaze for long. "Unless you'd like to mutiny. Anyone want to try me?"

"No, captain." A murmur passed through the crew, and they dropped their gazes.

"Good," the captain said. "Now back to your posts. I'll need all hands for this." She turned back to Zarah. "Miss Remei, guide us."

Zarah stepped to the bow of the ship, closed her eyes, and raised her hand toward the fog. The captain moved aside, giving her room and authority. "Forward. Slowly, but forward."

"You heard her, boys! Slow, but don't stop." The captain's voice rang out across the deck, and the crew hurried to obey.

Alaric held his breath as they passed into the Veil, half expecting a crash or burst of magic. But the Veil was only fog, cool and wet on his skin, his clothes, his hair. Soon the ship passed into an eerie blindness. There was soft white light in every direction. Nobody spoke. Even the sounds of footfalls on the deck were muffled.

"To the left, just a little." Zarah said.

"Port, and not too hard!" the captain called out. The crew moved in an instant, and the ship began to veer to its left. Alaric felt the motion in his legs and in his gut. It was a welcome change from the serene oblivion of the fog.

"Keep left," Zarah said, her eyes still closed. "Be ready to turn right when I say."

"Keep it to port but be ready to turn starboard on my mark," the captain called.

"Right! Now!" Zarah said. "Hurry!"

"Now!" the captain shouted. "Hard to starboard!"

The ship lurched hard to the right, and Alaric barely kept his footing. He heard a yelp from Maxime and the small cry from Professor Lamarca. Rook stood at the wheel, nerves and sea legs steady.

"We have avoided the reef." Zarah's voice sounded far away and strange to Alaric. It wasn't quite like someone else was speaking through her, so much as she was speaking someone else's thoughts. "It is just below the surface, and sharp enough to sink a ship this size. A pirate vessel learned that the hard way thirty-two years ago. Three sails and twenty cannon could not save it."

"Zarah?" Alaric asked.

"Forty men, a pet monkey, and three great island tortoises," Zarah said. "Their bones lay below us, picked clean by ocean scavengers."

Alaric shuddered. Zarah couldn't possibly know the things she was saying. Something was speaking through her.

Gorvin leaned over the railing. "Forty men? How does she know that? How can she know that? I can't see a thing. This is madness!"

"And how is this fog still here?" Behir asked.

"There's wind for our sails." Gorvin raised up to stare at Zarah. His voice rose in volume, pushing through the quieting mist. "It should blow the fog away. It's unnatural. This is a ghost fog, a devil fog."

"Silence, blasphemer!" Zarah pointed at Gorvin, but the voice that shook the deck was not hers. "Heaven's Tears formed these islands and the mist that guards them. Do not sully them with your defiled mouth."

Gorvin stood ramrod-straight, his eyes as wide and wild as a drowning man's. "What did you call me?"

"Calm down, Gorvin," Behir said. "Don't trust the girl. Trust the captain."

"Calm?" Gorvin's wild hair formed a shaking mane, and his wiry form tensed like a cornered cat's. "Calm? We're blind! We're all blind out here. Everyone except that girl, and she's mad. Or worse, possessed."

Behir grabbed Gorvin's arm, but he shook free and stomped toward the prow. "How are you doing this, girl? What are you doing to us?"

If Zarah heard him, she gave no sign. "I care nothing for your threats, only blasphemy." The voice came from her mouth, but it was not her own.

Alaric stepped into Gorvin's path. The wild-haired sailor hadn't looked so big before. His fear and rage made a giant of him.

"You need to stop." Alaric realized he was standing like the first mate showed him, poised to move, ready to act.

"We're going to die because of you!" His friend Lirrin rushed up beside him, his eyes rolling wildly.

"Hey!" Behir stepped forward. "Stand down. We can talk about this!"

"You!" Gorvin shouted at Zarah and Alaric. "You two got us into this!" He pulled back his fist.

Alaric raised his hands to defend himself. Nikolos was right; sometimes he couldn't run away. Not with Zarah right behind him in a trance.

Gorvin swung, but the hard punch never landed. A thunderous open-handed slap drove the sailor to one knee.

Nikolos Mordos stood over him, empty-handed but no less dangerous. "Get ahold of yourself, sailor, or I'll throw you overboard, and it will be forty-one drowned sailors on the reef below."

Gorvin knelt there for a moment as the fear-rage drained from his face. "I'm sorry. I don't know what came over me."

"See that it doesn't happen again," Nikolos said. "You get one slap. Next time it's steel."

Gorvin nodded.

Lirrin rushed forward and shoved Behir out of the way. He almost reached Zarah but found Damia instead. She grabbed his arm and drove him face-first into the ground. "Stay still or I'll snap it right out of joint."

Behir cried out, stumbling back into Rook and sending the ship's wheel spinning. Both men hit the deck in a tangle, and the ship lurched to the side.

Alaric watched in helpless shock as the Scarlet Gray plunged off course and into the mists. The world went white as the mist covered the deck. He found his way to Zarah as much by feel as by sight.

"Zarah, what's going on?"

"Miss Remei?" The captain shouted, "Report."

"We're off course," Zarah said.

"You sound like yourself!" Alaric grinned, despite their situation.

"I can't hear the World Flower," Zarah said, "I'm on my own."

"What do we do?" Lamarca and Maxime stumbled over toward them.

"I don't know," Zarah said, "I'm not getting anything. No word, no visions, nothing."

"We wait," Jill said. She stepped closer, moving by sound, her red coat and hat just visible through the mist. "We can't sail blind, so we wait."

"For how long?" Lamarca asked.

"As long as it takes," the captain said, "we can't find our way without her."

Chapter 11

Mists lay heavy all around the Scarlet Gray. Though the world looked no different than it had moments ago, Alaric felt the shift. They were directionless, suddenly lost. From their reactions, everyone onboard felt it, too. A murmur went through the crew, then a tense, plaintive silence. The air lay utterly still, as if the world had stopped. Even the ship's swaying diminished.

"What do we do?" Rook asked. "I've got control of the wheel again, but I can't see a thing."

"We wait," the captain said, "get some rest if you can. Eat if you're hungry. There's no telling how long we'll be here."

Nikolos and Damia prowled the decks, watching the sailors with narrowed eyes.

"I don't like this," Alaric whispered to the professors, "The sailors are afraid of being lost here, but they're more afraid of Nikolos."

"It's working," Lamarca said, "That may be all we can ask for right now."

"Pressing down one fear with another always has a price," Alaric said, "I've learned that the hard way."

One nervous hour later, the Shrouded Sea relented. Zarah stepped to the prow of the boat. "The World Flower has spoken. We have gone astray because of our own fears, and we have lost the confidence of the World Flower, but we are to be allowed one more chance. We will chart a course to three islands. On each island, we will be tested. Those who persist and survive will be allowed to seek the world flower again."

"Survive?" The word murmured across the sailors' lips. "Survive?"

"Going off-course out of fear was a deep offense," Zarah said, "only because the situation is desperate are we allowed an opportunity to regain our place. Be thankful for what we have. Now, ahead, and slightly to the starboard."

"You heard her," Jill said, "get moving."

Zarah guided the ship through the thick, maddening mists, until suddenly the shroud lifted, and they found themselves in a circle of blue sea surrounding an island of lush green. "This is the first test."

The captain looked through her spyglass. "Any word on dangers?"

"No," Zarah said.

"I'm not going to ask whether that means it's safe or whether that means you're just not going to tell me," Jill said, "I think I already know the answer. Alaric, here's your first chance to prove yourself. Be useful on this island, don't put us in any danger, and show that you're a valuable member of my crew."

"Thank you," Alaric said, "I will."

The captain scowled. "Don't make me regret this. Cross me, or act the fool, and I'll leave you on the island."

Jill looked at the island one more time to her spyglass. "I see birds, plants I recognize, rocks, a sandy beach. It just looks like an island. I know looks can be deceiving, especially here. Two boats, including mine. That's fourteen people. Myself, the passengers, and Rook.

Hannibal bring three sailors. Nikolos, bring Damia and two of your wolves."

"Aye, captain."

The sailors did as their captain ordered, and soon rowed into the peaceful bay of the island. They pulled the boats up onto the white beaches, and sweet scent of flowers met them. The sun shone warm, making Alaric almost forget the damp cool of the mists.

Alaric looked up and down the beach, then into the woods. The lush green blurred into the background as he sought out threats. The skills he'd developed on the docks and the back alleys meant little here. He had no idea what form the danger would take, and whether to look high or low to find it.

"It's beautiful," Alaric said, "I don't trust it."

The captain chuckled. "You may have some sense after all, boy."

If their wide-eyed gazes and laughter were any indication, the other sailors didn't feel the same. They didn't seem to feel the same knot of tension, as if something were watching them, as if they were only waiting for the ground to explode beneath their feet, or for spiders to rain down from the sky, or spears to come flying from the woods. They looked happy, peaceful, even a bit drunk.

"Have they been drinking?" Alaric asked.

"No, of course not," Jill said.

"Maybe there's something in the air, then. This island is a test, after all."

The sailors spread out across the beach, pointing a coconut trees and the island's green interior. Only the sea wolves seemed concerned. Their hands hovered near their swords, and their eyes scanned the forest. Nikolos, Damia, and their two men kept ready while the other sailors split up and explored.

They spent the next half hour walking around the island. The sailors gathered a half-dozen kinds of fruit, found two streams of clean water, and caught sea cucumbers and urchins out of the tide pools.

Nobody ate anything, not yet. They hurried back, excitedly, to the professors.

"Come on," a red-haired sailor said, "tell me this is safe. If it is, this place is paradise." He bit his lip like a child in anticipation.

Lamarca examined their haul. She cut open coconuts and mangoes and pineapples and thick, starchy bananas. She sniffed at them, dug the seeds out, and eventually tasted them.

"These are all recognizable, known plants," Lamarca said, "they taste the way they're supposed to taste, and I can detect no abnormalities. They should be safe to eat."

A cheer went up from several sailors, until a glare from Nikolos silenced them.

"If that's true," Rook said, "this island could keep the crew happy and well-fed for the rest of our lives. I'm sure there's good fishing in the water." As he said that, a silvery fish jumped broke the waves, and splashed back down. "I reckon that would taste good grilled over a fire."

"Forever?" The red-haired sailor asked, "You mean we could live here?"

The words spread among the sailors like a fire across dry grass.

"We could live here?" A scarred, blonde man said, his eyes wide and wild.

"It's beautiful."

"It's paradise."

"Hey!" Hannibal's voice called, "Captain, you need to see this!" He stood just around the bend of the beach, just above the line of the high tide, sheltered from view by rocks. In the center of that natural shelter stood a little hut made of wood, thatched with leaves that had long withered.

"What is it?" Nikolos asked. His hand hovered near the grip of his sword.

"A shelter," Hannibal said, "but there's a dead man inside."

The assembled sailors went silent. Alaric felt the weight of their anticipation, their worry. He could almost hear the questions in their mind: Is this paradise safe? How did he die? Will we die, too, if we stay?

"Let me look at the body," Maxime said. He stood looking into the shelter for a moment, then knelt down. "He's decomposed down to just a skeleton, but look, his clothes are mostly intact, and his bones are lying as a man would sleep."

"What does that mean?" The captain asked, "How did he die?"

Maxime pulled the clothes away from the body slowly, looking at each bone carefully. "Step out of my sunlight. I don't want to move the body, but I need to see." He looked again, examining the clothes and where the body lay. "I see no signs of violence. There are no marks of a stab into the bone that didn't heal, no bite marks. The color of the hair, the thinness of what remains, the stooping in the back, and the condition of the teeth, all indicate an old man. I think he died of old age."

"Convenient," Nikolos didn't look down at the professor, but scanned the woods with his eyes, keeping his hand near the hilt of his sword.

"There's something else his body tells us," Maxime said, "Something even more relevant to this island's safety."

"Spill it," the captain said.

"There are no large scavengers or meat-eating animals of any sort on this island."

Rook laughed. "How do you know?"

"His bones have not been moved. His clothing is mostly intact. Anything large, like a pig, a dog, or a wolf would have scattered his bones and gnawed them. After he died, his flesh was eaten by birds and insects and perhaps crabs, but nothing larger, nothing capable of dismembering the body. And that means nothing large lives here that eats meat."

"Do you know he was not poisoned?" Nikolos asked.

"I do not," Maxime said, "but my colleague found no sign of poison and no sign of danger in the fruit that you all found. I do not see a source of poison. Perhaps a snake or stone fish, but we have not seen any evidence of those. We have evidence that he was very old when he died, which implies that he lived here safely for quite a while. And we know that his body was largely undisturbed."

A palpable sense of relaxation swept across the surrounding sailors. Alaric felt it like a wave across his shoulders, a turning of the tide, and strangely, a danger rising.

"It's safe?"

"It's safe! This island is safe!"

"That means it's paradise!"

"We can stay!"

Two sailors ran back to their landing place and signaled the Scarlet Gray. They jumped up and down, shouting and waving.

"Stop that right now!" Jill said, "Would you like me to maroon you here?"

"Yes," one of the sailors said.

"Aye, captain," the other added.

The captain looked back at her ship, and saw three more boats launching, full of laughing sailors. "Oh, drown it to the depths."

Jill Crimson stood staring as three boats full of grinning sailors rowed from the Scarlet Gray to the island. She held her spyglass like the hilt of a sword, her knuckles growing pale. Alaric tried to think of anything he could say to her to reassure her, but even he couldn't find a good way to spin this. Even without a spyglass, he could see the Boatswain, Collum, shouting at the sailors to stay.

"This is not good," Maxime whispered, "she's losing control of her crew."

"Wait. Let's see how far this goes," Lamarca said, "She's resourceful."

Alaric looked at the captain, then at Zarah and the professors. "I hope you're right, Lamarca."

When the boats hit the beach, the sailors ran onto the shore, wide-eyed, with none of the caution the first crew had. Alaric didn't know many of them, but he recognized Gorvin, Lirrin, and Behir. "Those three caused this," he whispered, "maybe we should leave them here."

"Precedent," Lamarca said.

"Sailors!" The captain shouted. The men stopped and turned to look at her. "Why are you here? I didn't authorize this."

"They waved to us," Gorvin said, "We thought that was the sign. And look at this place. It's like paradise."

"We could resupply here," Lirrin said, "or maybe even -"

The captain cut him off. "I assure you that if Hannibal needed help resupplying, he'd have called for men himself. And he'd have had you leave enough room on the boats for supplies."

"Look at this place!" Behir said, "Surely after all we've been through, you wouldn't deny us a look at paradise."

"It's an island," Jill said, "it's safe, as far as we can tell, but there's nothing magical about it."

"Exactly," Lirrin said, "We're going mad in this blind sea. And now she says we might not even survive? We might not even get to the Island of the World Flower?"

"That's your fault," Alaric said, "You three panicked and threw us off-course."

"Brave boy," Lirrin said, "big words."

Nikolos growled at him.

Lirrin turned to look at the big man.

"What I told your friend goes for all three of you. You get one slap, then you get steel. And Gorvin already took the slap."

"I'm sick of getting threatened," Lirrin said, "None of us are safe with those wolves onboard."

"That wolf is my brother," the captain said.

"That makes it worse."

"What are you saying? You want to stay?" The captain asked.

"Yeah," Lirren said, "we do."

A bashful murmur passed among the sailors. "Aye." "Yes." "I do." "Sorry, captain."

"Sea wolves," Nikolos said, "surely none of you wants to stay here."

Damia and the two sea wolves said, "No! We will not stay."

Nikolos chuckled. "Well, I've done my part. My people are staying on. And these three will give no more trouble, if they value their lives."

"Very well," the captain said, "Crew, you're grown men, and can make your own choices. But men of honor stand by their agreements. We all agreed to this. We made a promise to Miss Remei and her people to see them to the Island of the World Flower. We agreed to this job, and that means seeing it through. I will not be staying, and I'll not look favorably upon any who do. I can't make you rejoin my ship. Especially not this many of you. I'll not put a gun to your head or a blade to our throat. But crew, remember who you are, and remember the promise you made."

Rook Corbin bowed his head. "You're right, captain. I may be too old for this, but I'm not too old to keep my word. Is anyone else with me?" He walked over to the captain, bringing one more sailor with him.

"That's it? You all want to stay?" The captain asked. Her voice cracked just a bit at the sight of nineteen men looking down at their feet, nineteen men abandoning her without even looking her in the eyes.

The sailors murmured among themselves, but no more of them moved.

"Permission to address your crew, captain," Alaric said.

"Granted."

"If you stay here, this is it," Alaric said, "This is all you get. A comfortable life, as comfortable as this island can give you, with each other for company. And if that's what you want, if that's why you joined the crew of the Scarlet Gray, then that's what you can find here."

"Sounds good to me," Gorvin said. Nikolos silenced him with a glance.

"What I'm offering you, what your captain is offering you, is a chance at greatness," Alaric said, "It's not just the money, though there will be money enough to live like kings. No, more than that, it's the renown and the respect of being part of the crew that found the treasure that people have sought for decades. This treasure has passed into legend, and most have given up on it."

"If it even exists," Behir said.

"We're here, aren't we? In the Shrouded Sea," Alaric said, "We're in the unbelievable. We have a chance to find that unbelievable treasure and bring it home. A chance to go to the Island of the World Flower, to see sights that no living man or woman has ever seen, to do things that no one on the mainland believes possible. To see those things and perhaps return alive. If you stay here, you're giving up greatness for comfort. You are giving up wonders for coconuts, sea cucumbers, and mangoes."

"Tell me the truth," Behir said, "Do you believe in this treasure? Or were you just spinning tales to get what you wanted?"

"A month ago, before I met Zarah, I didn't believe the Heavenly Courts, the High King of Heaven, the Shrouded Sea, or any of this.

I thought it was all just a scam the priests set up for the temples to make money. Nobody really believes that anymore. But since then I have seen things beyond my comprehension. I've seen things that make me believe again. Scary things. Things that make me wonder if the Divine wants me dead, but real and powerful things. We are here in the middle of the Shrouded Sea. All of the tales are true. Are you going to stop here? Where's your hunger? Where is your thirst for glory and wonder? Don't you want to see what comes next?"

A murmur passed among the men, and seven more walked over to stand beside their captain, including Behir.

"Looks like that silver tongue of yours was valuable after all, Alaric," the captain said, "as for the rest of you, I can't believe I'm losing a dozen sailors. But if that's your choice, it's your choice. I'll leave you one boat, in case you need to go out for fishing. But we're taking the rest back. I'm disappointed in all of you, but the Scarlet Gray will persevere. We've suffered losses before. We won't let this stop us. Goodbye, men."

"I can't help thinking the island won that one," Alaric whispered.

"It took a quarter of my crew without spilling one drop of blood," the captain said, "you're drowned sure it won."

"Worry less about the twelve we left behind, and more about the next island," Zarah said, "we must reach its lagoon and survive. Desertion is the least of your worries."

Without another word, those returning to the ship loaded themselves into the boats and rowed offshore. Alaric sat between Rook and Zarah.

"If the other islands take that kind of toll, we'll be skin and bones by the time we reach the big island," the old sailor said, "losing twelve sailors will make life a lot harder on the rest of us."

"We'll have less margin of error, to be sure," Alaric said, "I'm sure there are more dangers to come."

"Less margin, and longer shifts," Rook said, "We're twelve down, but the same work has to be done."

"It's worse than that." Alaric ran through the numbers in his head. "Nikolos has twelve sea wolves, including himself and Damia, right?"

"Right."

"And until now, there were thirty-six sailors, not counting the sea wolves," Alaric said, "and we just lost twelve of them, so we're down to twenty-four."

"Also right."

"So, there were three sailors for each sea wolf," Alaric said, "and now there are two."

Rook took a long breath. "When you say it like that, it sounds bad."

"Any ambitions Nikolos have are going to seem a lot more reachable now," Alaric said, "I know the captain is his sister, and family matters, but numbers matter more."

Chapter 12

They set sail from the first island. The absence of the missing crew lay like a second fog across the Scarlet Gray. The ship seemed hollow and empty, though there were still thirty-six sailors and four passengers on board.

A few hours later, the Scarlet Gray sailed in sight of the second island. Alaric had grown accustomed to the salty air, but another smell carried across the breeze. He wrinkled his nose. "Flowers."

"They smell good to me," Rook said, "the heat drives their scent along."

"Do you smell what's beneath them?" Alaric asked.

Nikolos growled. "Death."

Rook glanced at him, then at the scholars, then at the captain. "Maybe I'd best sit this one out."

"Perhaps you should," Jill said, "I'll need you at full strength later. This island will try to kill us. I need my brother's wolves."

"I say." Maxime pointed at a pair of deep blue spots in the shallow water, flanking their path into the island. "Are those blue holes? I've read about them, but I've never seen them before."

"Blue holes?" Zarah asked.

"Deep caverns in the sea floor," Maxime said, "that's why they're so much bluer than the sea around them."

"I heard they're all connected," Rook said, "That there's a maze of tunnels beneath them, and terrible creatures swim through."

The captain snorted. "I doubt we'll find a sea serpent."

"Oh, no captain," Rook said, "Not a serpent, a losca. It's half octopus, and half shark."

Jill chuckled. "I'll take that under consideration. Since there are blue holes here, that means the lagoon we saw is probably a blue hole. It won't be safe to drink. Inland blue holes have fresh water on top, but beneath it's salty, or worse, contaminated with whatever's down there. We'll drink what we bring ourselves."

"Good idea," Maxime said, "the island is trying to kill us, after all."

Alaric, Zara, the scholars, Nikolos, and Damia rowed with the captain in her landing boat. Six sea wolves followed in a second boat. The water near the island was shallow, clear, and calm. A half-dozen small stingrays played in the gentle waves, and red crabs scuttled along the sea floor.

They landed on a sandy beach and pulled the boats ashore without difficulty.

"This feels too easy." Damia looked around them, her hand hovering near her sword. "I thought this island was going to try to kill us."

"There's still time," the captain said.

"Hey, what's this?" Alaric stared at a large stone that rose up just in from the beach. "It's some kind of carving." He looked over to another large stone. "There are more here. And here. All the large stones have them."

Maxime hurried over. "Fascinating."

Lamarca joined him. "I haven't seen anything quite like this before. Have you?"

"No." Maxime drew a piece of paper and a charcoal pencil from his robes and made rubbings of each carving. "Assuming these aren't ruined, I'll try to piece together an interpretation." He frowned. "Not that I have any of my books with me."

"Come on," the captain said, "we know we need to reach the lagoon. This island is going to try to kill us. We may as well face it now."

The walk inland from the beach was too easy. Damia and Nikolos looked around them like cornered beasts, their hand hovering over the hilts of their swords. Alaric felt it, too, the sense of being watched, of lurking danger.

Trees dotted the small island. Coconut trees grew throughout. As they moved inland, evergreen and deciduous trees became more common. Alaric didn't know most of their names. He thought one might be a pine and another some sort of oak. It hadn't mattered what the trees were called back in Port Theron, and he'd had too many other things to remember to learn their names.

Lamarca passed by each tree, saying its name, remarking on the soil composition, and how such trees could even have gotten here. "It's hardly possible that they could have blown in on the wind, and I don't see how they could have been carried by birds."

Alaric hadn't seen a single bird overhead or on the land, nor any beasts ashore, aside from a few insects buzzing between the trees.

"There it is," the captain said, "the lagoon." It lay ahead of them, a round, peaceful, deep blue circle.

"That's our enemy? That will try to kill us?" Nikolos asked. "Very well." He drew his sword and advanced on it. Damia and the six sea wolves did the same.

When the first man reached the edge of the water, tentacles burst through the surface, grasping arms full of suckers. The sea wolves cried out and swung their swords, slashing at the fast-moving, slippery things.

Then the massive jaws of a great white shark rose up, big enough to bite a man in two.

"The losca?" Jill drew her sword and advanced. "I thought that was just one of Rook's stories."

Alaric started forward to join her, but Zarah held him back with a strong hand. "Stay here. If nine warriors can't stop it, we'll have to figure out another way."

"I'm not afraid," Alaric said.

"We'll need your wits, not your strength," Zarah said, "Please."

"Fine, I'll stay."

Nine blades slashed against the suckered arms, but the creature was too fast. It slammed one of the sea wolves back, then ripped the sword from another's hand. Two more rushed forward, but the losca knocked one aside, then grabbed the other and drug him toward its massive jaws. The bearded man struggled against the tentacled arms and pushed his shield into the creature's mouth. The losca bit through the steel buckler, but it bought the sailor the moments he needed.

Nikolos and Damia lunged forward, slashing at the tentacles. Damia's sword cut deep, and Nikolos's massive broadsword severed a suckered arm entirely. The losca shrieked in pain and tossed the sailor through the air, slamming him into a coconut tree. His arm twisted and broke.

"Retreat!" The captain shouted, "We can't win this way."

The fighters hurried backwards, slashing to block the creature's grasping arms, struggling to avoid being dragged into its jagged jaws.

"What if it comes out of the water after us?" One of the sea wolves asked. "I've seen octopi come on to the rocks after crabs."

"Then we'll fight it on land," Damia said.

But it did not follow them onto land. The losca did not leave the safety of its blue hole. Perhaps the half of it that was shark prevented it. Perhaps it knew they'd have to return.

The sea wolves stood, catching their breath, helping their fallen friend up.

"Your arm's broken," Jill said, "we'll put it in a sling. I'll need you to wait at the boats."

"Aye, captain," the sea wolf said through gritted teeth.

"He must be hurting pretty badly if he isn't arguing," Lamarca said.

"Drown it! How are we going to beat that thing?" Damia asked.

"I don't know, but there's more than one way to pass a test." Jill looked at Alaric. "Did you hear that boy? You're going to have to figure this out, or we're all going to die here."

Maxime took the charcoal tracing of the three sigils out and held them next to each other. "I still don't know what these mean. But if there are others in the island, perhaps we can put the meaning together."

"There are other rocks," Alaric said, "let's see."

They searched the island, keeping well clear of the lagoon. Hardy, thin grass clung to the dirt, but aside from the scattered trees and bushes and a few rocky outcroppings that burst from the sandy ground, little else could be found.

"This rock has something on it," Alaric said, "It just looks like the losca."

"It does." Maxime took a charcoal rubbing of it just the same.

Zarah frowned. "I can't feel the World Flower here. I can't feel anything."

Alaric found another carving. "This one looks like a monkey."

Lamarca and Maxime descended upon it.

"That's not a monkey," Lamarca said, "it's bigger, like an ape. Maybe a baboon or a gibbon?"

"I don't know what those are," Alaric said.

"Are they dangerous?" Zarah asked.

"Anything here is bound to be dangerous," Alaric looked around, glancing behind trees, back the way they'd come, but saw nothing.

Then he heard it, a sound like the hammering of fists on chests. Then a whooping, yelping, howling, gibbering cry echoing all around them.

"To arms!" Nikolos shouted. Everyone who had a sword drew it. Even Zarah clenched her fists.

A crowd of sand-colored apes rushed out, emerging from bushes and behind trees. They stood about four feet tall, running on their long arms and short hindlegs. They wailed and gnashed their teeth, long and pointed enough to tear flesh.

Nikolos met the first one and slashed it across the chest, sending it tumbling backwards. Damia struck the head off of another. The sea wolves lunged into action, slashing and stabbing, but the horde kept coming.

One of the sea wolves yelped as his sword was twisted from his hand. He'd stabbed it through an ape's chest, and the creature pulled away, bleeding sandy soil, the blade entangled in vines.

"They're plants!" Zarah shouted, "They're part of the island! We can't kill them."

As if in confirmation, the ape Damia had decapitated rose up, a new head forming from vines and sand.

"Run!" The captain shouted.

Nikolos charged at the thinnest point in the apes' line. He and Damia punched out at once, and the creatures fell back, creating an opening. They all ran through it. The apes charged after them, hooping and gibbering, flanking them in a wide line that brooked no turns.

"They're herding us!" Alaric said.

"There's nothing to be done about it," the captain said, "just keep running."

As the apes grew closer, two of the sea wolves turned back to fight them. They fell beneath the stampede. The apes ran over them, leaving them where they fell. Alaric had only a moment to hope they were merely unconscious.

The sounds of the apes echoed behind them, but never closed in. Every few minutes, another cry, and another thump sounded out as another sea wolf turned back to fight and was overrun.

Alaric's sides burned. His breath came in shallow panting. His vision began to tunnel. And in that tunnel, rising up from the stone of the island, he saw a cave mouth. He dragged Zarah toward it. The sounds of gibbering and the fall of lost sailors drove him forward.

He burst into the cave and tumbled forward into salt water, landing half submerged. His head swam, and he closed his eyes tight as light sparked behind them. He braced for impact, for the final assault of the apes, but instead found quiet, broken only by the breathing of his comrades and friends.

Alaric opened his eyes, and saw Zara, the scholars, the captain, Nikolos and Damia. Only they had made it into the cave with him. The apes stood at the mouth of the cave, silent, almost motionless.

"Are they dead?" Damia whispered.

"The apes are just waiting," Zarah said, "I don't need the World Flower to tell me that."

"I mean my friends," Damia said, "the sea wolves."

"I didn't hear any death-cries," Alaric said, "When I glanced back, I didn't see the apes stop to finish them. If they survived the initial attack, they're probably still alive."

"You don't know that," Damia said.

"No, he doesn't," Jill said, "and neither do I. But I know that we're in saltwater. I know that these caves connect. I know that the losca is out there. I know we're in more danger than they are, even back there with those apes."

Damia nodded. "Do you think there's a way out?"

"We have to go down into that," Alaric said, "the water's only going to get deeper."

"These islands are tests," Zarah said, "There will be a way out, if we can pass the test."

The captain lit a lantern. "Until we have to swim, we may as well be able to see." She and Alaric led the way deeper into the cave. Zarah and the scholars followed close behind. Damia and Nikolos brought up the rear.

"I'm surprised Nikolos isn't out front," Maxime whispered.

"Maybe he's afraid the apes will charge in behind us, and he will have to stand against them while we escape," Alaric whispered back.

"Or maybe he's afraid the losca will attack from the front," Zarah whispered, "And he doesn't want to be the first eaten."

The water rose or the cave descended. The stagnant saltwater smelled stronger, with a faint rotting seaweed scent. It was first at their knees, then their thighs, and then their waists. The captain held the lantern at shoulder level, its light almost blinding in the still darkness of the cave.

"If only I could make sense of those glyphs," Maxime said.

"One looks like the losca," Lamarca said, "one looked like the apes, but what about the first three?"

"Let me see them," the captain said. "This is a shark's tooth. This is an octopus sucker. These just refer to the losca. These are from the beach, right?"

"Yes, but there's this third one," Maxime said, "it just looks like two arrows going in opposite directions."

"Perhaps we have to figure out how to separate the losca," Alaric said.

"Separate it?" The captain said, "from what? The water?"

"A shark is almost helpless in on land," Nikolos said, "as deadly as they are in the water. And an octopus, although they can survive briefly on land, and occasionally even hunt among the rocks, would never hunt something the size of a human out of water. We've already seen that the losca does not willingly venture onto land. If we could beach it somehow, I believe we could kill it."

Lamarca frowned. "What if we have to separate the shark from the octopus?"

"How? Why?" Nikolos asked.

"Because this is a test," Alaric said, "and I doubt the island wants to test our ability to swing a sword. The reason we're even facing this test is fear. We went off-course because some of the sailors panicked and lost track of what they needed to do. I've been afraid, too. I'm not trying to say I'm better than they are. We all know I'm not. But that's what happened, and that's why we're here. And that's why the men back there are hurt or worse. Because of fear. And I don't think the island cares how good we are at sword fighting. I don't think the World Flower would test us on that."

"He's right," Zarah said, "whatever skills in battle you have, they may help us survive, but they are not what the World Flower wants."

"Then what?" Damia asked, "since you know so much, since the world flower speaks through you, or since you speak for it."

"It has spoken through me, but I've never spoken for it," Zarah said, "I think if we survive, we must do it with courage and ingenuity. Alaric's right. It doesn't care how good we are at fighting."

Nikolos frowned. "Then how is this possible? How do we win?"

"Those ape-things herded us here," Alaric said, "this is the critical part of the test. It's here in the next few hundred feet that we live or die."

"Looks like we've got another test right here." Jill held up the lantern and pointed. The path split before them. One showed light and seemed to lead upward. The other led deeper into darkness.

"The only sane and sensible path is the one out of this pit," Nikolos said, "but I know what you're going to suggest."

"If I've learned anything so far," Alaric said, "it's that the World Flower doesn't like easy solutions."

Nikolos nodded. "We must go into darkness. The only hope of the doomed is victory. The only path to life is death." He smiled grimly. "We Solok know about lost causes."

"Then into death we go," Jill said, "and hope we emerge into life."

They followed the dark path downward, until the water lapped against Alaric's chest, and he had to work just to breathe against its cold weight.

"Look, up ahead." Alaric pointed at a glint of light flashing off the roof of the cavern. "Do you see that?"

"It looks like another symbol," Maxime said, "it looks like a gem."

"It's reflecting the light like a jewel," Jill said, "but it's just carved into the stone."

"Look at the whole glyph," Alaric said, "Doesn't that look like the surface of the water? At the top, above the gem?"

"It can't be that easy," Maxime said, "it can't just be a gem under the surface of the water, can it?"

"Easy?" Nikolos said, "Where do you think that gem is?"

"Under the water?" Maxime said.

"Where under the water?"

"The lagoon," Alaric said, "the gem is in the lagoon. The gem to separate the losca is guarded by the losca."

"And I think I know where that other cavern lets out," the captain said. "We've come to the end of this one, and we've found our answer. It's time to go and face the test."

The other cavern did indeed lead back to the lagoon.

"There!" Zarah pointed at the far edge of the water. "Sparkling in the sunlight. It has to be the gem."

"Who's going after it?" Alaric asked, "I can't swim."

"Neither can I," Zarah said.

"Nor I," Maxime said.

"Damia and I should stand ready to distract and fight the monster," Nikolos said, "I am an adequate swimmer, but I am a much better fighter."

"I can swim," Lamarca said, "I've never dived before, but I'll give it my best."

"Keep your robes on, scholar." Jill Crimson pulled off her hat, coat, and boots and dropped her sword belt to the ground. "Just keep that thing off of me."

Nikolos and Damia charged forward, swords out, splashing in the shallows to get the losca's attention. It rose up, massive jaws wide with rows of teeth, suckered arms lashing like whips. But as soon as the captain hit the water, it turned away from them.

"It knows what we're doing!" Alaric ran into the shallows, shouting and throwing stones at the losca. "Come on, island! You know who I am! I know you want to kill me."

The losca turned toward him for a moment. Its dead shark eyes met his, and some flash of recognition arose in them.

"I know you hate me. I know this whole island, this whole sea hates me. You want Zarah to get through, but you don't want me. Well, I'm right here! Come on!"

The losca hesitated, but then turned towards him. Two massive arms reached out and grabbed Alaric's chest. He dug his feet into the shore but found himself being dragged slowly into the creature's massive jaws.

Nikolos and Damia rushed forward, slashing with their swords. But the losca's other arms whipped out, driving them backwards, pinning their arms.

Zarah rushed forward and shoved a coconut into the shark's mouth. It bit down, smashing it into pieces, swallowing part of the husk and spraying coconut milk everywhere.

Maxime and Lamarca joined in, grabbing rocks and coconuts and even a fallen shield to drive into the creature's mouth.

With every bite, dust, coconut milk, shards of metal, and broken, jagged teeth sprayed onto Alaric. And with every bite, Alaric drew closer to those cold and merciless jaws.

Alaric closed his eyes, then opened them. "Oh no. If I'm going to die, I'm going to watch it happen." He smelled the creature's breath, the stench of rotting flesh, oddly mixed with the sweetness of fresh coconuts.

Just before the jaws closed in on him, the captain broke the surface holding a sparkling gem in her hand. "I've got it! Now let him go!"

When the sunlight hit the gem, a red glow burst across the lagoon, filling Alaric's vision. Though he could not see, he felt the arms releasing and the jaws retreating.

When his vision returned, a small shark and a fair-sized octopus swam lazily in the waters of the lagoon.

"It's not even that big," Alaric said. Then he fell to the ground.

When Alaric came to, a cool breeze was blowing across the island. Zarah knelt beside him.

"That was very brave," she said.

"Don't get used to it," Alaric said, "I'm a survivor at heart, and that involves a good bit of cowardice. Are we safe? Did we pass the test?"

As if in answer, the remaining sea wolves limped to the edge of the lagoon. Some were bruised, others injured, and a few had to be helped along by their comrades. But they were all present, and all alive.

"Yes," Zarah said, "only one island remains, only one more test to pass."

"Will it try to kill us?" Alaric asked.

"Not exactly." Zarah frowned. "Not like this one. But it will be the most dangerous test of all."

Chapter 13

Scarcely an hour out from the Iosca's island, the Scarlet Gray pierced the mists around the third and final island. Dark vines covered a maze of stones haphazardly strewn, as if broken and shaken by some great catastrophe or by the hand of the Divine.

"This is our island," Zarah said, "we must face its trials if we are to continue."

Two boats launched from the Scarlet Gray, carrying fourteen souls to the island. The rocky beaches gave them safe harbor. There were no bones scattered about, no poisonous snakes or wolf prints. A few insects buzzed here and there, and a few crabs scuttled around the shallow water. No birds flew overhead or nested in its rocks.

"Where to, Miss Remei?" The captain asked.

Zarah led them to the tumbled-down rocks. "Here." She brushed aside a bit of green and showed seven marks on the stone. "Seven may enter. Seven must pass."

"Is this a maze?" Alaric asked.

"A labyrinth, a maze, a test," Zarah said.

"I won't send my crew where I won't go," Jill said, "and we won't pass the test by waiting." She led the way, followed by Nikolos, Damia, Zarah, Alaric, and the scholars. "The rest of you stay here and keep an eye on the boats. Don't leave us behind."

"Aye, captain."

Vine-covered walls rose up on either side of them, even as the path sloped upward, until they blocked the view of the ocean and shaded the path. The sun beat down hot from directly above, but the green-covered walls lent a chill to the air. The path traveled straight ahead for perhaps twenty feet, then turned right for another ten, narrowing as it went.

Suddenly, the path opened wide, into a nearly square room.

"This isn't natural," Lamarca said, "it's too square. Nature forms perfect, regular shapes from time to time, but not like this. This could be a ruin, perhaps an ancient temple, reclaimed by the forest."

A floral scent, with hints of vanilla and musk filled the air.

"What's that?" Alaric asked.

"My mother's perfume," Maxime said, "I believe this test is mine." He frowned. "I'm not entirely certain where to begin."

"Maybe with this?" Alaric pointed to a flat space of rock where the vines had retreated from. "What gain is loss?"

"What gain is loss?" Maxime chuckled. "My entire academic career. I was a second son, the spare. My only real job was to stay out of trouble and be ready to take over if something happened to my older brother. And preferably to father sons in case my older brother didn't. That was it. But I just had to let my dilettante interest in history and archeology and folklore grow into an obsession, and then worse, into an academic career. With each accomplishment, my family was less pleased. But in the end, my brother had two sons, an heir and a spare of his own. So here we are."

"Is this what this island wants," Alaric muttered, "for us to spill our sad stories?"

Damia scowled. "Have some courage, boy. Own your scars and be thankful it's not trying to kill us yet."

"So where does that leave us?" The captain asked, "I still don't see a way out of here."

Maxime paced the perimeter of the unnatural square, his brow furrowed, his fingers folded. "Wait, there was a story in the ancient Raeti culture, I think. A princess had been captured and placed into a labyrinth. The king offered great rewards to any man who could free her. Meanwhile, a young farmer wanted to marry his love, but had no money. So, he gathered what little he had and set out to free the princess from the labyrinth."

"Is this going somewhere?" Damia asked.

"The trick to enter the labyrinth was a false wall. There was a gap, but the wall beyond it was a perfect match to the wall, so that knights and nobles' sons passed by without even realizing the entrance was there. The young man from the farm wanted to find his fortune and marry his love so much that he beat on every inch of the wall until he found the gap. Humble determination succeeded." Maxime reached out and grabbed hold of the vine-covered wall. "Help me find it."

Within a few minutes, he had found a gap in the wall, cleverly concealed by perspective and the perfect alignment of the vines and stone with the wall of the passage beyond.

"That's some workmanship for a bunch of plants and rocks," Alaric said.

Jill frowned. "This is better work than our wheel locks, and I paid a pretty coin for them."

"Let's see where it leads," Zarah said.

"Hey, professor," Damia said, "Are you going to finish the story or not? What gain was loss?"

"The farm boy found the princess and returned her home. But the reward was to marry her and become a prince."

"All that effort, all that work, and he'd be forced to marry someone else," Zarah said, "Nobles are trash. No office, Maxime."

Maxime chuckled. "None taken. The king was so insulted that the boy didn't want to marry his daughter, that he gave him no reward, but instead kicked him and slapped him and drove him out of his castle. He returned home with bruises, a ripped shirt, and even less than he'd had before. All he gained was loss."

"It could have been worse," Damia said, "He could have lost his head."

"I suppose he could have," Maxime said, "that wasn't really a part of the story."

"He was weak, and he trusted people with more power than he had," Damia said, "abuse and death are always a part of that story."

Damia led them through the false wall gap into a long passage that curved to the left, roughly following the wall to the previous room. The passage led to another room with six openings, each half-obscured by hanging vines. Different flowers burst from each section of vines; white, orange, yellow, red, violet, and blue. The smell of dried flowers and chemicals fill the air.

"I think this is mine," Lamarca said, "it smells like my childhood experiments and my current lab."

"I found your question," Alaric pointed to a portion of stone with vines brushed aside. "What does the wise woman know?"

"Wise woman?" Lamarca frowned. "Being called a wise woman is like being called a local folk healer or a hedge doctor. It's not a compliment for a woman of science."

"Nor for a woman in leadership," Jill said, "And yet that is the question it offered you."

"Then I'll answer," Lamarca said, "My story is unsurprising. Nobody wanted to hire academic tutors for a girl, much less let her into the university, much less make her a professor, but I was undeniable. I worked twice as hard as my classmates, achieved twice as much, and only got the minimum of grudging respect. As I said, unsurprising." She chuckled.

"I know the story too," Jill said, "not many women helm ships."

"What isn't as clear is how lonely it can be," Lamarca said, "to be excluded from the collegial spaces, to be told again and again that you don't belong or that you're taking a space that a man should have. And when people are finally willing socialize, finding it's impossible to get past the rejection and resistance they've shown. That loneliness is not as well known." She smiled just a little. "But the wise woman knows that it's worth it. It's worth every lonely struggle. Every one."

The captain laughed. "I'll drink to that."

"So where does that get us?" Damia asked, "I don't see a way out."

"I suppose we could try each path and keep notes as to where they go," Maxime said, "but that approach does not work in the old legends."

"Ships that sail blindly break themselves against reefs and rocks," Jill said, "We'll not make that mistake."

"We have six exits," Alaric said, "We just have to figure out which vines to move."

Nikolos grumbled. "Which vines? They're everywhere."

Lamarca frowned. "The wise woman. What is wrong with this island, to ask me about the wise woman?"

"I don't know, but if you answer, we can move on," Damia said.

"The wise woman is also a character in many stories," Maxime said.

"I know," Lamarca said, "It's just insulting to be stuck in that role after all I've learned and done. Fine. The wise woman knows the next step the hero must take on his journey. But this story's hero is not a he. Zarah, those flowers are Northern Hydrangea. They're native to much colder climes than this one, more like your home. Try pushing them aside."

Zarah pushed the thin white flowers aside, revealing another passage in the rocks, so narrow that they could only walk one at a time and Nikolos's broad shoulders barely fit. When they emerged, they found themselves in a circular space with little room to spare.

Across from them stood a passage leading deeper into the labyrinth.

"That looks too easy," Alaric said.

Vines grew across the way they'd come and the exit, trapping them. A sharp smell filled the room that smelled green to Alaric.

"That's me," Zarah said, "that's the smell of my garden, the prickly green smell of the squash vines in the summer and the beans just getting ready to be picked. There's a little bit of the soil there, that rich northern soil. That's mine too. Go ahead and ask your question."

Some vines brushed aside on nearby rock, revealing the words, "What will you not give to stop this plague?"

Suddenly, visions filled Alaric's senses. A band of farmers played lively music on old and handmade instruments, accompanied by the rhythmic stamp of dancers' feet. He smelled old hay and fresh sweat and felt the heat of a barn filled with dancing men and women. He saw Zarah there, dancing with the boys from her village. He saw one in particular, as tall as she was, but a bit thinner, with just the beginnings of a moustache. The boy liked her, and she felt the same.

It hit him like a shock, seeing Zarah in such a normal life, dancing with a boy, laughing with her family and friends.

The vision swam, and the air grew cooler. In a modest farmhouse, a wood fire burned in the hearth. Zarah and the boy, now fully grown, gathered with their families to welcome a baby, Zarah's baby. Then, he saw the child growing up, joined by another, and another. Then he saw Zarah, with thick streaks of gray in her hair, in that same modest farmhouse, welcoming her first grandchild.

The vision broke, and Alaric's senses returned to the island labyrinth. He staggered a bit, seeing the potential life, and lives, that would now never be. "Zarah." He whispered her name but could think of nothing else to say.

"What would I not give?" Zarah asked, "Nothing. You know that. My life, my future, my mind, my soul. I can't give another's life. It's not mine to give. But all I am and have is thrown on the fire. Even if I go home alive, what will be the same? How dare you even ask that?"

Damia whistled low. "I hope this island doesn't hold a grudge."

But the vines pulled away, revealing both the entrance and the exit.

"The World Flower doesn't care if I'm angry," Zarah said, "only that I obey. Now come on. It's getting late."

As Alaric followed Zarah down the passage, he felt a chill cross his back and a weight in his gut. "Visions. This island showed us visions. It's not showing visions of my life. Not if I can help it."

The passage led around a curve and into another squared off section, a room of sorts. The smell of coffee filled the air. The stone simply said Alaric. The way they'd come in and two other walls had paths leading out. The remaining looked like a solid wall of leaves and rock.

Alaric. The word was as plain as the gray stone. The air lay still and heavy.

Alaric felt his gut twisting, a weight settling in his chest. "What do you want?"

As if in answer, the edges of Alaric's vision began to blur, and a memory of early childhood started to form, a tiny, lonely child. Alaric could feel the gnawing in his tiny belly and the mouselike fear in his eyes.

"No!" Alaric shouted. "No! You will not flay my life open for your amusement!" He shook his senses free from the memory, ran for the nearest wall, and jumped. His hands found holds among the vines and rocks, and his feet followed. Soon he stood atop the wall.

The visions stopped, and everyone turned to stare at him.

"Alaric, what have you done?" Zarah asked.

"I found the exit," Alaric said, "There's a false wall exit there. I'm assuming it's the right one, since it's hidden." He hopped down. "Let's go." He walked out without waiting for a reply.

Zarah ran up behind him. "That was foolish."

"I'm better at climbing than self-reflection," Alaric said.

"You won't be able to escape that reckoning forever."

"But I did today."

At those words, thorns grew from every vine. Some were short and bristly, others as long as a knife blade. The thorn vines crept over the top of every wall and hardened from bright verdant green to a wintry brown.

"Maybe not," Zarah said, "You won't be able to do that again."

Chapter 14

They emerged from the passage into a thorny, narrow clearing. Even the rocks seem to jut out aggressively. They had to stand shoulder to shoulder to avoid the knife-like barbs.

"If I get stabbed because of this," Damia said, "I'll have my revenge. If I have to drag myself out of the grave to do it. You should have let that vision play, boy."

"Easy for you to say," Alaric said, "It wasn't your life." He pointed to the stones. The question 'Where do you go when the mountain crumbles?' was carved in between the thorns. The air smelled of onions and pipe smoke.

Damia growled in the back of her throat. "That's mine. No need for tricks or visions, island. I'll tell my own story, thank you, and I'll tell it true. If I lie, or leave something important out, you do what you have to do."

As if in answer, the vines slackened just a bit.

"You see me, six feet tall and eyes two different colors. They tried to call me a witch. Boys my age tried to beat me up. But boys my age weren't as big or as tough as I was. They didn't call me a witch twice. Eleven years old, I thought I was the queen of the world. I could whip any boy my age or even a little older. I never had a father to protect me, and in my mind, I didn't need one. He died not long after I was born. We didn't have to scrimp to buy things. My grandparents made sure we never went hungry and always had a place to live. Mother didn't even remarry until I turned twelve.

"By then I was a wild and fierce thing, and my mother was running out of time to have more children, which she desperately wanted. So she found a man. He was good enough, I suppose. My stepfather wanted me to marry. Not at twelve, but by twenty, and he set about trying to make me into a lady. I didn't appreciate that, and I pushed back every chance I got. I even threw hands at him once. But just once. I was already four inches taller than he was, and I thought I could whip anyone. That night I learned that even a tall girl is nowhere near as strong as a full-grown man. I'd never been beaten in my life. I'd never been beaten like that to be sure. That night I packed up some food a couple of knives and some money my father hid away for me, and I was gone before dawn.

"I ran from town to town, looking for somebody who could teach me to fight a man. I found a swords woman who taught me the basics. She said my two-colored eyes and my height were signs from The Lord of War that I was to be his warrior. She called me Damia Two-Eyes and taught me the blade.

"I did all right fighting gladiatorial fights, blunt weapons, demonstrations. But I knew even though I was better, better than I'd ever been, that I still didn't have what I needed. I could feel the danger, when a big man bore down on me with all his strength. I needed more skill, more sharpness. I knew how to fight. I needed to learn to kill. Then Nikolos saw me fighting and saw my potential. He took me on as a student and taught me to kill men. And now I fear no one. Not long after, the captain saw us in port. We shared stories over a cup of some awful bitter sludge that she loves."

Jill chuckled in mock offense. "How dare you insult my coffee?"

"We found out that she and Nikolos have the same father, and we've been on her crew ever since."

"That's great, but where do we go?" Zarah asked.

"To answer the question on the stone," Damia said, "I was the mountain. When my world crumbled, I went to the sea."

"The sea?" Nikolos said, "But it's all around us."

"There has to be a path here," Damia said, "Our swords could find it."

Nikolos smiled and drew his sword.

Alaric watched the two of them walk toward the nearest wall of vines, blade drawn. They slashed out, catching the thorny vines against the stone and severing them. Alaric looked around for signs of retaliation. "I've got a bad feeling about this."

"Then draw your blade and help us," Damia said, "You're the reason we're in this spot."

Alaric reached for his machete, but his hand hesitated. "There has to be another way. Where is the sea from here?"

"All around." Damia paused. "But also down. Here, look. This path goes down."

Alaric walked the path. "I think you're right. This does slope down."

"It better, boy," Damia said, "I'm passing through thorns because of you. This could have been flowers." She stepped toward the hanging vines where Alaric stood.

"I didn't think you were the flowers type," Alaric said.

"Watch your mouth, kid," Damia said, "Just because you heard the short version of my life story doesn't mean you know me. Now shut up and follow." She pushed the thorn vines aside and vanished into the labyrinth.

As Alaric followed, he noticed blood on the thorns. He started to speak, but Damia silenced him with a two-colored glare. He slipped to the back of the group, farthest from Damia.

"Do you wish you'd answered the question now?" Zarah asked.

"No," Alaric said, "I don't want this island to push me around like that. I'm willing to endure a bit to stand my ground."

"You're not the only one suffering," Zarah said, "That wasn't your blood on the thorns."

The passage as it sloped down and curved to the right. Hanging vines clung to every surface, deep green and studded with thorns. The air smelled of salt, and the shaded rocks sweated. Moisture dripped down vines to pool on the stony ground below. The slick ground felt treacherous, as any misstep could send them stumbling into the vines' sharp embrace. Finally, they emerged into a broad open space. Vines grew across the walls and the floor. Across the way, not twenty feet away, was another opening.

"Eyes open," Jill said, "Anything this easy is bound to be a trap."

The air grew suddenly dry and cold, bringing the smells of blood and urine.

"This one is mine," Nikolos said. "There, on the rocks. What will I say to my father when I meet him?" The big man chuckled. "I will tell him my name, and who I am, and then I will kill him." He stepped toward the exit. "Defy me if you dare, island."

As he stepped, the vines wrapped around his ankles. Nikolos drew his sword and slashed downward, cutting the vines aside, but with each step, more vines came. As he stalked forward and cut, a vision burst forth.

A young woman as pale and dark-haired as Nikolos fell to her knees, begging. Her ice-blue eyes were bloodshot, and tears flowed down her pale cheeks. One hand cradled her pregnant belly, while the other reached out to a massive man who, except for his gray eyes, could have been Nikolos. He turned and walked away.

When vision passed, Nikolos had cut halfway across the field of vines. The big man found his rhythm, slashing and stepping before the vines could regrow. "Yes, we all know he left us. He left my pregnant mother alone, and me fatherless." He slashed down faster, severing vines in front of and around him. "But don't just show her weakness. Show her strength. Show the things she did so we would survive. Show the steel in her gaze. Show the man she killed to protect me. She begged once, then she fought like a she-wolf for the rest of her life."

The island's response was rapid and violent.

"Look out!" Alaric shouted. A vine shot up from the ground and wrapped around Nikolos' sword-arm. He quickly drew his knife and slashed the first vine. But another vine grabbed his knife hand. He pivoted his hips and brought the sword in close, severing that vine. He slashed down at his feet but could barely keep up with the attacks.

Another vision rushed in, a young boy with black hair and ice-blue eyes, running from older boys, crying, stumbling, tumbling down a hill to lie in a heap in the gully below. Four older boys stood atop the ridge, laughing and throwing clods of dirt down at him.

"Nikolos?" Jill whispered, "Oh, my brother. I never knew."

"That is not who I am! Show the rest!" Nikolos roared and slashed with his knife. He bit down on a thick vine, tugged it loose, and burst free from their grasp.

The vision began again. The same young boy stood cooking a simple meal of porridge. His mother staggered into the house, dark rings under her eyes. Though Nikolos could not have been more than seven years old, his mother looked two decades older than she had. She sat down heavily, and he placed a bowl before her.

"Thank you, Nikolos."

He reached his arms around her shoulders and held her while she ate. "I'm sorry you're sad, Mama."

She forced a smile and said, "How could I be sad with a son like you?"

Nikolos snarled and slashed at the vines that held him, rage fueling his sword. He started making progress toward the exit.

The visions wavered in and out of Alaric's senses for a moment, as if struggling to overcome Nikolos' fury. Finally, the island won out.

The four older boys from before surrounded Nikolos. The shortest of them, a ginger brat with oversized teeth, held a trembling baby rabbit.

"Leave that rabbit alone, Gurtos!" Nikolos said.

Gurtos laughed and squeezed harder.

"Stop! You're going to kill it."

"No," the tallest of the four boys said, "You're going to kill it."

"Harkot, no," Nikolos said, "Please."

The boys erupted in laugher at the word please. "Kill it! Kill it!"

"Break its neck with your hands and we'll leave you alone," Harkot said.

"You'll leave me alone?" Nikolos whispered.

"Yeah," Harkot said, "You'll still be fatherless, but at least you won't be gutless."

Nikolos reached out and took the rabbit. It didn't struggle. It just trembled in his hands. One snap and it would be dead, and he would be … "No." Nikolos turned and ran, putting on a burst of speed that surprised even him.

"Hey! Gutless brat! Come back!" Gurtos shouted.

They bigger boys gave chase. Nikolos got far enough ahead to hide the rabbit, then led the boys back toward the village. But that delay was all they needed to catch him.

They beat him and called him gutless for standing up to them. The irony and stupidity of the situation was little comfort.

"By the depths!" Jill's voice broke through the vision. "Is that why you won't eat rabbit?"

That night, Nikolos limped and winced as he struggled to get supper together. When his mother walked in, the fatigue left her eyes, replaced by an urgent worry. She bandaged his wounds and finished preparing the meal, even bringing out the last of the dried fruit as a treat.

"I couldn't let them hurt that innocent little rabbit," Nikolos said, "And I wouldn't do it myself. Why do they have to be like this?"

"You see that our world is cruel and violent," His mother whispered, brushing a strand of dark hair back from her young son's face. "You are a good, kind child. Perhaps somewhere in the world that would be welcomed. Not here. Here, you must decide how much you are willing to suffer to stay kind and good."

That night, Nikolos lay awake. First he thought, staring intently at a space on the wall. Then he cried, mourning the child that he was. Then he planned. Finally, he slept.

By dawn's first light, Alaric saw the same boy, his pale face bruised purple, his breath showing in white puffs. His hands trembled as he placed two fist-sized stones in his jacket pocket, then grabbed two more from the ground.

The same four boys came back. They surrounded him, laughing and jeering. "Fatherless brat." "Half-orphan pig." "Your mother is _"

The last insult was cut off by an explosion of violence. Young Nikolos' right hand swung up, catching the boy in the mouth with the stone. He staggered back, spitting blood.

The boy to Nikolos' right grabbed his hand. His shock turned to anger and outrage, the way bullies always do when their victims fight back, as if the four boys were suddenly the victims. In his outrage, he forgot Nikolos' left hand. It swung around in an arc, driving its stone into the boy's eye. He fell to the ground, grasping the side of his head and crying.

That left Harkot and Gurtos standing. They both lunged forward to grab Nikolos's arms. He struggled for a moment, but they were bigger. Even with all his rage, Nikolos couldn't shake them both.

Gurtos wrenched the stone from Nikolos' hand twisted his arm behind his back. Nikolos couldn't break free, so he bit down on Harkot's finger until he tasted blood. The boy cried out and let go. Nikolos pulled the rock from his left pocket, spun around, and punched Gurtos in the stomach. Gurtos cried out and fell to his knees. Nikolos swung again, and knocked Harkot to the ground.

The vision ended with seven-year-old Nikolos raising two stones against two wounded older boys, standing over the prone forms of two more.

"By the Heavens," Maxime whispered, "You were a child."

The vines paused for a moment, as if waiting for an answer.

"I became a man that day," Nikolos said, "I learned to defend myself."

"What happened to those boys?" Lamarca asked.

Nikolos shrugged. "I didn't kill them, but I made sure none of them ever forgot my name. And if their memories grow hazy, they have their scars to remind them."

"Did you get in trouble?" Zarah asked.

"For what? For beating four older boys?" Nikolos laughed. "That was the first thing I ever did that my people approved of."

"I'm so sorry you had to go through that," Lamarca said.

"It made me strong," Nikolos said, "That day attracted the attention of a swordsman. He taught me to fight, to really fight. That's why I'll never lose, because I am the swordsman, but I am also still the boy who turned his fear to rage and broke the ones who'd hurt him."

"Our father did this to you," Jill said.

"Huh." Nikolos paused for a moment, frowning. "I see what the island wanted of me. Very well, island, I will admit it. When I see my father again, I will thank him for making me strong. Then I will kill him for what he did to my mother."

"I don't want you to kill our father," Jill whispered.

"Then pray we never meet."

Chapter 15

The passage curved back to the left briefly, then brought them to a long, open space. The exit lay diagonally across from where they stood, perhaps forty feet away. The sun shone bright and hot in the open space, but thick, lush vines clung to the stone walls.

"Don't even try to cross yet. This a trap," the captain said.

"Of course it is," Alaric said.

The wall began moving, blocking off the exit.

"Alaric, I believe this is yours." The captain said.

I don't smell coffee," Alaric said, "I smell smoke, maybe gunpowder?"

"Drown it all, it is mine," Jill said, "What? No visions? Not going to rip the memories from my head?"

"No," Zarah said in a distant, hollow voice, "this you must choose."

The vines pulled away from the stone, revealing the question, "Why do you hate pirates?"

"Might as well answer." Jill glared at Alaric. "No need to antagonize the weeds further. Pirates are a constant danger to our lives and profits, and I'd never want to be one. Living on the run and dying young isn't the same as living free."

The vines on the walls grew spikier. Others pulled back, revealing jagged rocks beneath them.

"What?" Jill asked, "Every word I said was true."

The wall moved toward them, and the exit slammed shut.

"Move it!" Jill said. They all hurried to the far edge of the area to avoid the jagged rocks and thorns. The other wall had grown spiky too, and Alaric found himself standing tight between Maxime and Lamarca, tucking in his shoulders to avoid the thorns.

"It's half-true," Zarah said.

Nikolos and Damia stepped to the front and drew their swords, as if blades could shatter stone.

But the wall stopped halfway across the clearing, then slowly retreated, revealing the exit again.

"Come on, let's get out before it starts moving again," the captain said, "I've answered the question."

She rushed toward the exit, Nikolos and Damia close at her heels, but the wall surged forward again as soon as she got close, and they all had to retreat.

"Drown it," Jill said, "that's a dirty trick."

"Nothing this island does is fair," Zarah said, "it won't get better from here."

"Fine!" The captains said, "The first ship I sailed went pirate and got shot out from under me by the navy. It was almost a blessing to me. I was never going to make captain, or even first mate, on a ship like that. I lost good friends and shipmates, but a new chapter of my life began. A chapter that will never include piracy. I'll not let this crew die like that one did. This crew is mine to lead and protect."

Silence hung in the air for a moment. Then the wall rumbled forward, pushing further than it had before. It drove Nikolos and Damia back into the scholars. Alaric felt the thorns of the far wall pushing into his shoulder. He saw blood on Nikolos' face, and still the wall moved slowly forward.

"Drown it, Jill, you need to tell the whole truth before that thing crushes us all," Nikolos said, "Whatever you're hiding, just say it!"

"Fine. After I lost my first crew, I managed to sign onto another. These were pirates, but they were the only ones who'd take a woman.

We went a year without taking serious losses, and I earned my way to quartermaster. I thought I had the crew's respect, but then the captain got us into more trouble. He led us into a navy trap, and he and the first mate ended up dead, along with a quarter of our crew. We got away, but just barely. The crew chose a man for the captain, even though I was most senior. But worse, they chose a reckless fool, a man by the name of Gaun."

The wall stopped, but did not retreat, leaving them pressed shoulder to shoulder between stone and thorns.

"Gaun wanted revenge, of all things, and led us on more and more reckless missions. We took more losses, and the navy was closing in. So I did what I had to do to save my crew."

"What did you do?" Nikolos asked.

"I sold that fool to the navy in exchange for a pardon for the rest of us, on promise that we would leave piracy forever," Jill said, "I renamed the ship the Scarlet Gray and laid out my plan to the sailors. We'd sail the gray, carrying messages, cargo, and passengers other captains were too soft to carry, but we'd do it legally. No more running from the navy. No more dying in fire and salt.

"I lost half my crew that day, but I replaced them in time. And they lived on. That's more than Captain Gaun would have given them."

"You betrayed him?" Damia asked.

"One life for many," Jill said, "Maybe that's not a fair trade, but it's one we make every time we fight."

"So that's why you refuse me," Nikolos whispered.

"Aye, brother, because I don't want to lose you like I lost so many others. I committed treason and mutiny to protect a crew that were hardly friends. What would I not do for my own brother?"

At that, the spiked wall retreated fully and stopped.

"I guess the island is satisfied," Jill said, "come on. Let's see what it has in store for us next."

Nikolos lagged behind, with Damia. Alaric strained to hear what they said.

"I always thought I would be able to change her mind," Nikolos said, "but now, I do not think I will."

"What does that mean for us?" Damia asked.

"If we get that treasure, it means we will part ways with the Scarlet Gray," Nikolos said, "with my sister."

"And if we don't get the treasure?" Damia asked.

"I don't know," Nikolos said, "I do not know."

Zarah and Jill led the way into the next winding passage. As soon as they left the captain's trial, the smell of coffee filled the air.

"That's you, kid," the captain said.

"I don't understand," Maxime said, "We're not in a node. We're in a passage between nodes."

"Node?" Zarah asked.

"A room, for lack of a better term," Maxime said, "it seems wrong to call them rooms, when they're outdoors."

"Room or no room, this is my question," Alaric said, "Ask away."

Thorn vines shot across the path behind them, blocking the way to the previous room.

"You'd better pass this, boy, because we can't go back," the captain said.

"Those thorns are like daggers," Damia said with a grim laugh, "You've made our host angry."

More vines shot across the path, and the stone began to rumble. The path behind them began to disappear, churned up by jagged stone.

"Run!" Alaric grabbed Zarah's hand and ran down the path.

She stumbled after him, throwing him off-balance for a moment, then matched his pace. "You're going to have to fix this."

"How?" Alaric asked, "It's eating up the path behind us, and it hasn't even asked a question." The rumbling grind of the stone filled their ears as it devoured the path, and they had to shout to be heard above it.

"Maybe it's done with you, boy," Damia said, "I can't say I blame it."

"Look out," Alaric said, "dead end ahead."

"Left or right?" Zarah shouted.

They both looked the same, sharp stone covered by thorny vines.

"Right is closest," Alaric said, "Let's go."

They turned down the right passage. Alaric saw that it forked again, and rushed ahead to check the leftmost path. It ran him around in a circle and spat him back out where he'd started.

Maxime stared at him, wide-eyed. "A dead end?"

"A loop," Alaric said, "Hurry, maybe we can make it to the other path."

He ran back out into the main passage with the others close behind. He didn't spare a glance at the grinding destruction. The terrible noise told him all he needed to know. He sprinted for the path ahead and to the left, hoping the others could keep up.

Alaric slid into the passage, with Zarah and the Captain close behind. Nikolos and Damia ran in, dragging the professors behind them. The grinding stone and vines passed by their pathway's entrance, shredding the path and leaving a jagged stone wall behind it, dripping pulped plant matter, but still somehow woven with thorny vines.

"No time to catch our breaths," Zarah said, "it's coming."

As soon as she'd said the words, thorn vines grew across what had been the entrance to their path, and then the rocks began to churn.

"Go!" Alaric ran down the curving path before him, looking for a way out. The path curved sharply to the left, but never branched.

He glanced back. The professors were at the back of the pack, just barely outrunning the destruction. On instinct, Alaric turned back to look where he was going. The path curved more sharply than before, almost doubling back.

"It's a spiral." The captain slid to a stop beside him. "It was leading us here all along!"

Alaric glanced around the edge of the spiral. "It's ended. This is a dead end. A blind dead end. I didn't even see it." He shoved his way to the back of the group. "Behind me!"

Nikolos drew his sword, but the stones would not be cut.

"You've got us!" Alaric shouted, "I'm here. Ask your question."

The churning sound did not slow, and the far end of the spiral began to crumble.

"Come on! I'm ready," Alaric shouted.

"I don't think it cares anymore." The captain took a slow, deep breath. "I never thought I'd die like this. Still, it's better than being caught and hanged by the navy."

"What do you mean?" Alaric said, "Ask the question!"

"She means it's done. Over. You lost your chance." Damia's two eyes narrowed. "She means you doomed us all, you fool boy."

"No," Alaric said, "No. Island, if you don't have a question, I'll ask one of you. Please, have mercy! I made a mistake, but we're trying to help Zarah reach the island. We're trying to do the right thing."

The grinding wall of stone and thorns slowed but did not stop.

"It's toying with you, boy," Nikolos said, "No one ever got mercy just by asking."

Alaric took a step forward, until he could smell the pulped vines over the ever-present scent of coffee. "Fine. If you want a trade, take me, but have mercy on them. It was my mistake, my cowardice, that started this. Zarah needs their help to get to the island. Please, let them go."

The churning went silent, and the grinding wall stopped. Silence hovered over them for a moment, as if the island were considering Alaric's offer. Then the thorn wall melted into the ground, vanishing as if it had never been there.

"Are we safe?" Maxime asked.

"Yes," Zarah said, "The island has accepted your answer."

"How?" Maxime asked, "It never asked him a question."

"It didn't have to," Alaric said.

"It just had to almost kill us," Damia said, "I don't know if you were bluffing or not, but remind me not to play cards with you."

"I wasn't bluffing," Alaric said, "I didn't have a bad hand. I had no cards at all."

Nikolos clapped his shoulder, hard, and Alaric had to fight not to stumble forward. "Looking Lord Death in the eye," the big man said, "putting yourself between danger and your comrades? That's my boy. I'll make a man of you yet. Maybe not a swordsman, but a man."

"Miss Remei, is the test over?" The captain asked, "May we leave this island?"

"Yes," Zarah said, "we passed. I can hear the World Flower again, calling me. The fog will part, and the way made clear."

"Then let's go," Jill said, "I'm ready to leave this wretched place behind.

Zarah turned to the captain. "I trust you'll keep your crew in line this time."

The captain chuckled. "I will, if I have to clap them all in irons and row the boat myself."

"Good," Zarah said, "let's go. The Isle of the World Flower awaits us."

Chapter 16

Zarah stayed in her trance for hours, guiding them through the blind-white mists. Damia and Nikolos prowled the decks, but no more sailors lost their wits. Alaric stayed by her side, chilled by the ever-present fog. The hairs on the back of his neck stood on end, and his stomach twisted every time she spoke, but he stayed.

The mists darkened. Alaric wondered if night had fallen in the world beyond the Shrouded Sea. They sailed on, and in time the mists grew bright again.

Zarah came out of her trance with a roaring gasp. She staggered forward and slumped against the railing. As tall as she was, she almost tumbled over.

Alaric lunged forward to catch her. "Are you all right?"

Zarah nodded weakly. "Keep going straight. We're almost there. As soon as we're out of the mists, stop the ship. Don't wait. Stop it. Right then."

"Aye." The captain raised her voice once more and set her crew into action. "We're almost there, men! We'll emerge from the mists in a few minutes. When we do, drop anchor. Stop on the edge of the mists. No further until we know what we're up against."

The forward edge of the mist grew lighter and lighter until they burst out into dazzling sunlight. The sail dropped, the anchor chain rolled down with a grinding clank, and the ship lurched to a halt.

Alaric shaded his eyes and blinked until the island came into view. A central hill rose up like a tower, but taller than any building Alaric had ever seen. Vines and flowering plants and green of every shade covered it. The top of the tower looked to reach heaven itself.

Professor Lamarca stood staring. Her mouth opened first in shock, then in a wonderstruck grin. "Your folktales don't seem so ridiculous now, do they, Maxime?"

"No, they don't." Maxime stared up at the massive, green-covered tower and trembled. "Those old legends sounded ridiculous when I thought they were simple stories. Now that they might be true, they're terrifying."

"Terrifying or not, we're going in," Alaric said. "If there's a treasure or a cure on that island, we'll find it. No backing down now."

Zarah nodded. "No backing down now, no matter what it costs."

"Look alive, men!" Jill shouted. "We're not to the island yet. Stop looking up at that tower and keep your eyes on the sea."

Alaric looked over the railing. "What is that?" He stared at the twining patterns of green, like the knotwork on a Vorali broach. "Is that seaweed?"

"That's why I told you to stop," Zarah said.

No gulls squawked overhead, no fish splashed, but the seaweed writhed and undulated like the arms of a thousand squid.

"It's moving on its own," Alaric said. "How are we going to get through that?"

"We can't sail through that, Captain," Rook said. "Should I lower the boats?"

Jill frowned. "I don't know if the rowboats can get through, but we're bound to try. Launch my eight-man boat and the two sixes on the side. Rook, Nikolos, lead the side boats."

"Aye, Captain." Rook hurried off.

"Zarah, should we bring the wheellocks?" the captain asked.

"There's nothing on that island a gun will stop," Zarah said.

Jill nodded. "Machetes, then. Into the boats. Passengers with me."

Alaric, Zarah, and the professors boarded the captain's boat, along with three sailors he didn't know. The captain, Alaric, and the sailors all had machetes. Before he could ask why Zarah and the professors didn't, the boat dropped into the water.

Zarah trailed her fingers in the water, but her eyes were fixed on the tower. "We must climb the tower. Nothing can stand in our way. I must reach the top. Nothing else matters."

"Except the treasure," the captain said.

Zarah didn't reply. She kept her eyes focused on the tower.

"Zarah?" Alaric asked.

"The great tree of heaven must be put to rights. It must be made clean again. Wholeness and health must be restored."

"Zarah?" Alaric said. "Zarah!"

"Huh? Alaric? What's happening?" Zarah shook her head and blinked hard.

"You were staring at the tower and talking nonsense," Jill said. "That's what happened."

"The World Flower's call grows stronger," Zarah said. "I'm struggling to keep myself together. If I let up for a moment, it will overwhelm me. But in the end, it doesn't matter. What I have to do is more important than I am."

The captain shook her head. "I knew this journey was madness."

The thick, pulsing seaweed made way for the captain's boat, parting to reveal still water beneath. But the tendrils pushed back against the other boats. The seaweed tangled around the oars until they could not move forward.

"Enough!" Nikolos drew his machete and slashed at the seaweed. "We will get through!"

"Form up behind my boat!" the captain shouted. "Follow me."

Nikolos pulled a pole from the bottom of the boat and shoved it into the shallow water. He pushed off the bottom and drove the boat closer to the captain's. The sailors cut the seaweed free a little at a time, and bit by bit they fell in directly behind. The third boat did the same.

"Ahead, slowly," Captain Crimson said. "Pole the boats if you must." Her boat moved forward easily.

Zarah's gaze moved first to the water, then the island, then back, but she never really looked at any of it. Her sight lay somewhere beyond. Alaric wanted to shake her out of it, to ask her if she even knew where she was, but he didn't dare.

"Do you think she's all right?" Alaric whispered.

Lamarca frowned. "She's doing what she came to do. If she's right, she could save countless lives."

"You didn't answer my question," Alaric said.

"I don't' know. I don't know what this will do to her."

"Did you know this would happen?"

"Please understand, she came to us," Maxime said. "She was adamant, insistent. She all but forced her way into Professor Lamarca's lab."

"She was so sure, and we were so desperate that we couldn't say no," Lamarca said.

"No to what? What are you not telling me?" Alaric's voice rose. His throat tightened. "I told you to tell me everything."

"We told you what was ours to tell," Lamarca said. "Zarah told you what was hers to tell. But we don't know what's going to happen here. Surely you didn't think this would be easy or safe. We're all risking our lives, especially Zarah."

Alaric sighed. "It's easier to accept that danger for myself."

"Zarah is young. She should not have to do this. But the World Flower did not speak to us. It spoke to her. And so here we are."

She paused. "You're no older than she is. You shouldn't have to be here either."

"I want this," Alaric said. "I fought for this, and I'll keep fighting until I get my share." He glanced back at the other rowboats. "Speaking of fighting, I don't think they're going to make it."

Behind them, the sailors struggled to move. Seaweed regrew behind the captain's boat and blocked the others in. They cut and rowed and pushed and poled. Their muscles strained and sweat poured from their bodies, but they got nowhere.

"It's not working," Maxime said.

"Drown it!" Damia shouted. "I'm setting these things on fire."

"That would be unwise." The voice that came from Zarah's mouth did not sound like her own.

"Find us a way through or shut up!" Damia said.

Alaric shook her. "Zarah! Zarah!"

She turned to look at him, her eyes like the lightless depths. The green had almost completely vanished, her pupils had grown so wide.

"Zarah, do you hear me? Do you even see me?" Alaric shook her again.

Zarah breathed deep, like she was surfacing from deep water.

"Zarah?" Alaric asked.

"Thank you. It's getting harder. I'm not sure how much longer I can keep coming back."

"What can I do?"

"Talk to me." Zarah shivered, despite the heat. "Keep me here, in this world. I don't know if I can come back if I go that deep again."

"I will," Alaric said.

Damia pulled a lantern from her pack and lit it. Two other sailors lit lamps. The first mate stood waiting with his machete.

"Last chance," Damia shouted at the seaweed. "Move or burn!"

Green strands burst from the water. Damia and the sailors waved burning lanterns at them. The tendrils pulled back from the open flames, then burst out of the water like kraken's arms to attack the sailors.

Rook cried out as seaweed wrapped around both his arms. He grabbed hold of the boat, but the green dragged him toward the water.

Nikolos swung his machete again and again. Strands of seaweed flew into the air. But more of it came. It wrapped around his right arm and pulled it back. He grabbed the machete with his left and kept slashing.

The sailors on Rook's boat drew their machetes and cut him free. But the seaweed then wrapped around their arms, pinning their blades. It pulled one of the men into the water with a splash.

Damia slashed through the seaweed as quickly as Nikolos, then burned it with the lantern. Together, they kept the weeds from pulling any more sailors off. "Hah! I'll not be beaten by kelp!"

"Look out!" Lamarca shouted. "It's going to capsize your boat."

The seaweed grabbed onto the edge of Damia and Nikolos's boat. He slashed down into the wood, severing the tendrils. She swept the burning lantern, driving them back. But the seaweed kept flowing. It pulled down, and the boat leaned.

"We have to do something," Alaric said.

"Retreat! Back to the ship!" Jill shouted.

"We're trying!" Rook shouted. Seaweed dragged him toward the water.

"Zarah, is there anything you can do?" Alaric asked.

Zarah turned, and he saw terror in her eyes.

"Zarah, please," Alaric said. "They're dying."

Zarah nodded. "Goodbye."

Her eyes closed. When they opened again, they were shockingly green, inhumanly green. She spoke with a voice from somewhere far beyond. "World Flower! Listen!"

The seaweed paused, but it didn't let go.

"They'll go back to the ship if you let them go. Only my boat will go on," Zarah said.

"Your boat?" the captain said.

Zarah ignored her. "Please, let them go. I'll come to the island. I'll bring just enough people to help me reach you. Please, let them go."

The seaweed slid back into the sea. Rook and his crew pulled the sailor back into the boat. He coughed and spat up water for a few minutes.

"All right," Captain Crimson said. "Pull the boats up to mine. Nikolos, Damia, Rook, you're with me and the passengers. The rest of you, back to the Scarlet Gray. Alaric, make yourself useful and row."

A few minutes of rowing and careful stepping later, and the crew was set. The two side boats rowed back to the ship, and Captain Crimson's boat glided toward the island.

"Keep it slow." Jill held up her hand. "I suspect these weeds will let us through now, but we can't be too careful."

Alaric's muscles burned as he rowed, struggling at the unfamiliar task. "I don't think I can go much faster than this."

Nikolos laughed. "Slow and steady. Nobody's chasing us."

"For now." Rook glanced down at the seaweed. It looked perfectly peaceful now.

The seaweed parted before them as they rowed, opening a narrow path to the island.

"I don't like this," Rook said. "We only have one way in, and the seaweed is choosing it. What if it doesn't let us leave?"

"Don't worry about leaving." Zarah's voice echoed eerily across the quiet water. "The island will be glad to see you go. It's only calling me. It only wants me. Be more afraid of what will happen if you stay too long."

"Then let's be quick," the captain said. "We'll get what we came for and be gone before we wear out our welcome." They jumped out and pushed the boat ashore on a narrow beach. Warm sea water splashed into Alaric's boots.

"Pull her all the way ashore," the captain called out, "and tie her well."

"Do you think the seaweed would let it float away?" Maxime asked.

"If it does, who could rescue us?" Jill asked.

They beached the boat on a narrow strip of pale sand broken by hardy grasses. The full green began almost immediately. The beach itself wasn't long enough to hold the boat lengthwise. Nearly half of its hull lay on the tangle of wild grasses and ferns that reached to the edge of the sand.

A deep breath brought with it a dizzying array of smells: the salt of the sea, the rich odor of seaweed, the perfume of distant flowers, and the wet live smell of plants. It was as far from his home in the city as Alaric could ever hope to be. Here, nothing vanished into the background unnoticed.

In the profound silence, their every word and motion boomed. In Port Theron, Alaric had never known silence, even in the depth of night. Aboard the Scarlet Gray, the sounds of the wind and the ropes and the sails and the sailors filled every empty space. Here, only eight humans moved. No birds flew overhead. No sandflies buzzed around their legs. No crabs crept across the tide pools.

Jill's voice rang out across the narrow beach. "Stop standing around staring. We have a treasure and a magic flower to find, and I don't want to see this place at full dark. Get moving."

"You will find nothing on the beach, and nothing on the cliffs." Zarah's voice rang out hollow and strange, and Alaric understood what it had cost her to save the sailors. "We must enter the tower."

"No offense, Miss Remei," the captain said, "but I'll trust the eyes in my head over the voices in yours. Keep searching."

Alaric and Rook spent the next few hours exploring the island. They saw no insects, no snakes, no birds, no animals of any kind. They moved slowly, cutting only what they had to. In the end, the grasslands proved as empty as the beach.

"We should go back." Alaric looked toward the tower. It rose up in the center of the island, covered with twisted vines and bursts of flowers. "There's nothing here."

"Maybe the others found something?" Rook also glanced up at the green tower.

"No," Alaric said, "Zarah's right. We're wasting time out here. We have to face it."

Chapter 17

Alaric stood at the base of the massive green tower. He tried to trace the path of the vines that covered it, but they twined so tightly his eyes crossed. The scent of leaves and flowers mingled with the salt of the sea.

"Find anything?" Jill asked.

"Nothing," Alaric said. "No birds, no beasts, not even any insects. Nothing but plants."

"None of us did," Nikolos added.

"It's time," the captain said. "Zarah, please show us in."

"Here," Zarah said. Ahead, vines hung down like a curtain. Little flowers dotted the green with white, and gave off a faint, sweet smell. "Push them aside but be gentle." She vanished, passing through them like a ghost. Alaric followed.

The air grew cool and damp, filled with a thousand fragrances. The soil beneath Alaric's feet gave just a bit with every step, like the freshly tilled soil of a garden.

Rook looked around, his whiskered face trembling. He bent over and pulled off his boots. "I got the chance to stand inside a big tree once or twice. It's nice to be out of the heat, to be someplace cool and good smelling. But this is the biggest I've seen. There's something in the air here. This is holy ground."

To Alaric's left, at the very center of the island, a massive tree trunk rose. He craned his neck to see how far and how high it went, but he lost sight of it in the green above. Great limbs branched out in all directions, supporting a tangle of vines and leaves. "It's also dangerous ground."

Nikolos rumbled agreement. "I like the way you think."

Damia grunted and rolled her eyes. "Does this holy ground have our treasure?"

"We'll find it." Nikolos said.

"This island is not just a trial to survive," Zarah spoke in a strange voice, then went silent.

Alaric glanced from Nikolos to Zarah. Her eyes seemed brighter green than before. Maybe they were reflecting the foliage around her, or maybe the power of the island was shining through.

"Zarah?" He called her name, but she did not reply. "Zarah!"

Alaric couldn't shake the sense of danger. He felt the scholars' fascination and Rook's reverence, but fear overwhelmed them all. He looked left and right, above and below, searching for the threat, for the source of his unease, but he found nothing.

His eyes met the captain's briefly. She was doing the same thing, scanning, searching. She gave him a wry smile. "If I didn't know better, I'd think we weren't wanted here." Jill forced a chuckle.

"You aren't," Zarah said in a faraway voice, "You are tolerated for now because you are with the girl—with me."

"Then let's get moving. The sooner we get the treasure, the sooner we can be off this island. That will make everyone happy. I hope." The captain frowned. "Let's move."

Zarah led them onto a circular pathway woven from living vines and branches. It gave and shifted with every step. Alaric hurried to keep close to her. She walked quickly and with purpose, never worrying about the ground giving way beneath her feet. Alaric, on the other hand, noticed every motion.

"I feel it," Alaric said. "The island doesn't want me here. The green feels so alive it almost burns. There are parts of my soul that could not survive long in a place like this."

"You might be better off without those parts," Zarah said.

"What about me, Miss Remei?" Rook's pale eyes were wide and watery, as if the sights around were breaking them.

Zarah smiled. "The island hates you less than the others. You took your shoes off."

Maxime hurried forward and whispered in Alaric's ear. "I say, young Alaric. For a place that doesn't want us here, this island is making it easy for us to ascend. Too easy, I fear."

"It's making it easy for her to ascend." Alaric glanced over the edge at the long drop down. "If anything happens to her, this walkway might drop away. Then we'd plunge to our deaths."

Zarah chuckled in spite of herself. "Then you'd better make sure nothing happens to me."

"If it wants Zarah here, but doesn't want us," Lamarca said, "then we should be ready. It won't wait long to start picking us off."

"I don't see why you're so scared," Damia said. "They're plants. Not snakes, not lions, not warriors. Plants. What's the worst they can do? Augh! Stinking leaves!" She drew her machete, slashed through a low-hanging branch, and returned it to her sheath in one fluid motion.

"Do not anger the island," Zarah said. "Remember, you are not welcome here."

"Welcome or not, we're here," Damia said, "and we're not leaving until we get what we came for."

"If that is your wish, you may stay here forever."

Damia sneered. "Do your worst, plant-girl."

Zarah said nothing.

"Ha! I didn't think so," Damia said. "I'd love to see you try. Augh!"

Alaric spun around and saw the green reaching toward Damia. Her machete cleared her sheath in an instant, but vines caught her wrist, stopping her in mid-cut. The harder she struggled, the tighter they wrapped.

Alaric felt a moment's smug satisfaction that Damia had to eat her words so quickly. Then he saw Rook struggling against the same vines. His left arm was totally entangled. He cried out as the vines wrapped tight around his throat.

Nikolos's blade flashed out. He sliced through the vines, freeing Damia in an instant. Then he turned on Rook and cut him loose. Nikolos moved so swiftly that the captain had barely had time to draw her own machete and hurry to his side.

"What is this?" Nikolos held up his machete, and they all watched its metal drip away. Within seconds, its edge had been reduced to a jagged, useless crescent. Nikolos tossed the machete aside and held out his hand to Alaric. "I'll need yours."

Alaric frowned. He wanted to ask, "Why not take Corbin's? You said I was better than he was, and you just saved his life," but he knew no good could come of it. He frowned, drew his machete, and handed it to the first mate. "Here."

Rook patted him on the shoulder and whispered into his ear, "Neither you nor I could stop him if he turned on us. Not with blades, anyhow."

The spiral path continued upward. Alaric kept close to Zarah as much as he could. They walked for a few minutes, and then a burst of flowers in every shade and color imaginable broke the endless green above and ahead of them. Thousands covered an area the size of the Scarlet Gray's mainsail. The sunlight filtered through the flowers like a stained-glass window. Patterns of light and color fell across the ground and their faces.

"Extraordinary," Maxime said. "I don't believe I've ever seen that many colors in one place before."

"I don't think I've seen that many colors at all," Alaric whispered.

"I didn't know there were that many colors," Rook said.

"How is this possible?" Maxime asked.

"This is your area, Maxime," Professor Lamarca said. "Legends and miracles, not botany."

"I've seen this," Zarah said. "In my visions. We are on the right path."

"This wasn't in the vision you showed me," Alaric said.

"I've seen more than you have."

"This is real," Alaric whispered. "This is real. Does that mean the thorn men are real too?"

"You knew they were real all along," Zarah whispered.

Alaric did, but he couldn't think of them while he stared at the wall of beauty. The sunlight filtering through the petals cast the ground below in a shimmering mosaic, like standing inside a rainbow. Even Damia and Nikolos stood and stared. Even the warriors let down their guard.

Then the pollen burst.

"Duck!" Zarah pulled Alaric down to the ground. Low-hanging flowers popped, sending sprays of pollen into the air. Bursts of gold and pink and lavender exploded around them.

"What's going on?" Alaric shouted.

Maxime and Lamarca dropped and avoided the worst of the pollen. Even the little they inhaled sent them to the edge of sleep. Their eyes lost focus. They gritted their teeth and jammed their fingernails into their palms. They pounded on their chests, trying to stay awake.

"Down!" Jill shouted as she hit the ground. Her hat caught most of the pollen. It poured out the front corner in a stream of gold and pink. She shook it out over the edge, dropping the colorful powder far below them. "Drown you, Remei! Did you know this was going to happen?"

"I shouted duck as soon I knew," Zarah said. "We've got to keep going. The pollen fall will get us if we don't. Crawl. Stay low."

Rook, Damia, and Nikolos fell heavily to the path. Nikolos almost rolled off, but the captain pulled him back to the path before he could fall.

"Stay on the path, little brother." Jill scowled, then turned to follow Zarah. "I won't leave you, or my crew."

Alaric looked back down the path. Nikolos, Damia, and Rook had taken the full force of the pollen and lay facedown on the path. If not for the faint rise and fall of their chests, he'd have thought them dead.

"We have to get out of here," Alaric said. "We can't help them if we're asleep too."

"How will we help them at all?" Jill asked.

Zarah closed her eyes and pointed. "There. Those purple flowers are glowing. I think they're the antidote. But we have to get there."

"I'll be back for you, little brother," the captain said. "I promise."

Alaric glanced up and saw a row of swelling pods. He could guess what was in them. "Run!"

The pods burst, and streams of golden pollen burst out. Alaric pulled his shirt over his mouth and kept his head low, dodging the worst of it.

Zarah drove forward, her feet pounding the path like a raging bull. Alaric didn't know if the magic made her immune, or if she though the best way out was through, and he didn't have the breath to ask her.

He saw the captain beside him, running fast, relying on her hat for protection. But he couldn't spare a glance back at the professors.

More pods burst, and sprays of pink and green exploded outward. Alaric ducked lower. He could smell the pollen through his shirt. It was sweet, cloying, choking. It threatened to coat his throat and nose. The path seemed to swim in front of him, but he kept his eyes on Zarah and ran harder.

Behind him, he heard someone fall, then another. The captain was still beside him. It must be the scholars. They'd gotten dosed a bit to begin with. It must have slowed them, and the pollen caught them.

Alaric could feel himself slowing. The pollen was getting to him too. His vision blurred and doubled. He struggled to keep his eyes on Zarah.

Ahead, the purple flowers glowed in his hazy vision. His legs no longer burned with effort. Instead, they felt numb and heavy. Sleep. Sleep would be best. He could lay down his burdens, lay down his ambition, lay down his fear, and sleep forever.

He stumbled forward, his vision blurring to an indistinguishable mush of light and color. He felt a heavy hand on his shoulder, then something soft on his face, like petals. The sweet smell vanished, replaced by a sharp tang, like pine and wild garlic.

Alaric's eyes opened wide. He saw the world clearly again. Gold, pink, and green pollen filled the area, thick as the Shrouded Sea's mists. The professors lay sleeping on the path. They'd made it barely halfway to the flowers. A wide purple flower covered his face, the source of the strange smell. The same flowers covered Zarah and the captain's faces. They hadn't picked the flowers, but kept them on their long, graceful stems. He took care not to break his.

He sat, staring, for a long while as the pollen fell and the feeling slowly came back into his limbs. He tried to remember reaching the flower but couldn't. The world had blurred to light and colors. He's lost all sense of his body, save for a strong hand on his shoulder.

"Zarah?" he said from behind his flower.

"You were very close," Zarah said. "I pulled you the rest of the way. The captain too."

"Thank you."

Zarah shrugged. "It looks like the island doesn't quite own me—yet."

In time, the pollen stopped falling, and the air cleared. Perhaps the island gave up, or they passed its test. Alaric waited for Zarah to emerge from behind her flower, then followed suit.

"Pick three flowers, and only three," Zarah said. "One for Rook, one for Damia, and one for Nikolos."

"What about the scholars?" Alaric asked.

"They're light, and close." Zarah chuckled. "I'll bring them to the flowers, but I'm not carrying Nikolos."

Chapter 18

Alaric sat beneath the sunlit wall of flowers. The sickly sweet scent of the sleep pollen still gnawed at the edges of his mind, so he moved closer to the shimmering purple flowers Zarah found. Their musky, spicy scent drove the cloying pollen smell away.

The crew struggled to shake off the effects of the sleeping pollen. Nikolos stared at nothing, his eyes half open, sullen and silent. Even sitting down, he was massive. His face rested on one broad hand, pale skin against dark gloves.

Damia wobbled back and forth. Her eyes were everywhere, flitting from the path behind to the path ahead, from the flowers overhead to each crew member in turn. Alaric shivered when she turned her two-colored gaze on him. Her normally piercing eyes looked past him, glassy and drunken.

The scholars lay on the ground, holding their heads. Rook sat blinking. His white-whiskered face drooped.

"It's a good thing Zarah found those flowers," Alaric said.

Jill glanced at her crew, then back down the path. "No telling when we'd have wakened."

"Or if," Alaric said.

"You are not wanted here." Zarah sat beneath the shimmering purple flowers, her legs straight out, her body tense, at attention, her eyes distant.

"That's the island talking," Alaric said. "Come on, Zarah. I know you're still in there. You saved us."

Zarah's shoulders shrugged, and she sighed. "I'm still here, for now. But it's true. The island doesn't want you here."

"Can you tell the island we'll leave as soon as we get the treasure?" Jill asked.

"It heard you," Zarah said.

"You know, if the island would help us find the treasure, we'd both get what we wanted."

"If it were that easy, the island would have handed you the treasure when you got here. It doesn't care what any of us want."

"Well, I don't care what the island wants!" Damia slurred her words. She spat on the ground, and bits of gold and pink pollen sparkled in her spit. She braced herself with one arm. "Eh. I'm still seeing double, and don't blame my eyes. They worked fine before. Two colors, one vision. I hate this pollen. I mean, not really. It's interesting." She touched some pollen that had stuck to her sleeve. "It's powdery and soft and dusty all at once." She wrinkled her nose. "I don't like the smell though. Too sweet. These glowing purple ones are better. Spicy, tart, not sweet. I don't like sweet perfume. Bleh."

"Damia?" Rook asked, "are you all right?"

"I'd be a lot better if this island wasn't trying to kill us," Damia said, "or if my machete had a proper handguard. Why can't I get a machete with a proper handguard? If I try to punch somebody like I do with my saber, I'll break my little finger."

Alaric raised one eyebrow. If Damia was talking, maybe he could get her to say something useful. "If you find the treasure, you can have any kind of machete you like."

"Yeah. I'll have a machete with a gold-plated handguard," Damia said, "and I'll only eat sweet oranges. I'll throw out the sour ones, and never taste another lime again."

"Hear, hear!" Rook raised one hand like he was raising a glass. "Here's to oranges and lemons and no more lime juice."

The captain chuckled. "It does get tiring after a while, but it's better than getting scurvy."

"So, you like oranges?" Alaric asked. "Did you eat them a lot growing up?"

"When we could get them," Damia said. "Kumquats and satsumas grew wild, and we'd gather them from the woods, but they were never as sweet as the oranges. Those came from further south, and I loved them, loved them, loved them." She looked around, drunkenly serious, and turned her gaze back to Alaric. "Don't ask me to share my oranges, boy. I don't even share them with Nikolos, and we've been together for years."

"Together?" Alaric asked.

"Not like that," Damia said, "We're so much more than lovers. Lovers come and go. They cloud your mind and break your heart. You're better off without them. We're brothers in arms. Sisters. Siblings? Whatever. We've fought together a long time, kid."

"You told us this on the island," Alaric said, "We know you knew Nikolos before you joined the Scarlet Gray."

"Yeah, but he was looking for Captain Jill even then," Damia said. "When he finally found his sister, he said he'd only join the crew if I could come along too. And we've been here ever since." She spat another stream of saliva and pollen residue. "It must be the pollen. I get chatty when I get drunk. That's why I hardly drink."

"It looks like you're sober now," the captain said, "and our scholars are waking up too."

"Good," Zarah said. "Let's get going."

"One moment," Jill said. "I need to address my crew. We've been through real danger. If any of you want to go wait on the beach, now is the time. We very nearly died just now. I won't abandon our passengers, but the island clearly doesn't want us here."

"I'll do whatever you decide." Rook tugged at his throat where the vine had choked him. "But I was happy before we got this job, and I'll be happy if we walk away with our lives, treasure or no treasure."

"Gah! Coward!" Damia spat again. "I'm still not afraid."

"We knew we would face unnatural dangers." Nikolos's voice was little more than a low growl. His eyes still weren't quite focusing, but his mind was. "Who thought we could sail the Shrouded Sea and face only natural dangers? We're in an unnatural sea, on an unnatural island, seeking an unnatural flower. What did you expect?"

"You should go," Zarah said. "The island does not want you here."

"How about we split up?" Damia asked. "We could search for the treasure, and you search for your magic flower."

"Split up?" Rook said. "Wouldn't that be more dangerous?"

Maxime coughed and sat up. "It does strike me that the odds of finding and retrieving both the cure and the treasure are infinitesimally small. Perhaps we should focus on our main priority."

Lamarca grabbed his arm and whispered something sharply into his ear.

Maxime's face went pale for a moment, then relaxed. "Eh, I'm sure they'll make the right decision."

"Our main priority?" Nikolos said.

Damia smiled. It couldn't have been any more predatory if she had fangs.

"Wait!" Alaric shouted. He knew he had to think fast. "We can't do this. We can't split up."

"Why not?" Damia asked.

"This island doesn't want any of us here but Zarah. It just tried to put us all to sleep."

"I know."

"And the island is controlling her more with every passing hour," Nikolos said. "Don't think we haven't noticed."

"Zarah saved us," Alaric said. "If she hadn't found the flowers, we'd all be asleep. None of us had an answer. None of us had an escape. Only Zarah did."

"That sounds like even more reason to go back to the beach," Rook said.

"No!" Damia said. "The treasure will be ours!"

Nikolos nodded. "I didn't come here for a flower. The plague is not my concern. The world is wicked and cruel, and I won't lay down my life to save it."

"We can't split up," Alaric said. "We need her. You need her."

"The island doesn't want you here," Zarah said. "It doesn't care what you want. It doesn't care about your treasure. You should go back to the beach."

"No," Alaric said. "You need them too."

"What?" Zarah blinked hard. "Why? Wait. Stop talking through me, island. I'm here. I'm doing this. Leave me alone!" She turned back to Alaric. "Sorry. What?"

"Zarah, think. We need them here because of the thorn men."

"Thorn men?" Jill asked, "The songs say 'Thorun's Men.'"

"The songs are wrong," Alaric said. "Zarah's been having visions. She shared one with me."

"Shared? As in told you about it?" Rook asked.

"Shared, as in I saw it too," Alaric said. "The thorn men are made of vines and thorns. They're not friendly."

"Nothing on this island is friendly," the captain said.

"The island doesn't want you here. Isn't that obvious?" Zarah asked in her own voice.

"Zarah, we need them," Alaric said. "The thorn men are not of this island. Remember the vision? The island wants you here. They don't. You've had more visions than I have. Am I wrong? Think back."

Zarah frowned. "You're right. They're the problem. They're the reason the World Flower hasn't cured the plague already. It can't." She looked at the captain. "I'm sorry. I do need you. All of you."

"Why should we carry you?" Damia asked. "Why should we fight them for you?"

"Thousands will die if this plague is not stopped," Zarah said.

"Never mind that," Alaric said. "Do it because you need her. You won't make it through the rest of the island without Zarah. You need her to keep you safe from the island's defenses, like the pollen. She needs you to protect her from the thorn men."

"What about me?" Rook asked. "My fighting days are past, and even then I was never much of a swordsman."

"You can go back to the beach and watch the boat," Jill said. "I won't blame you. You're a good man and a good sailor. But I'm going ahead."

Rook sighed. "You know I won't leave your side, Cap. I'm in."

"Damia? Nikolos?" Alaric asked. "This is your best path to the treasure. Come on. You'll get to slice up some plants."

Damia laughed. "What do you say? I'd like the chance to cut some vines."

"Our best chance of getting the treasure is sticking together. For now." Nikolos stood slowly. "Are you all rested? Are we ready? I welcome danger, but I won't abide wasting time."

As they pushed themselves to their feet, Zarah leaned close and whispered, "Why were you questioning Damia like that?"

"She was talkative," Alaric whispered back. "She usually isn't."

"Why take advantage of her like that? She was drunk from the pollen."

"Damia is dangerous, like Nikolos. The more we know about her, the safer we are. If I can understand her, that's better still. I wasn't taking advantage of her. I was taking an opportunity to watch our backs. I don't trust them. You shouldn't either."

"Then why fight so hard to keep them near us?" Zarah asked. "If we can't trust them, why not send them away?"

"I told the truth this time," Alaric said. "Without them, we won't live long enough to be betrayed. The thorn men will kill us first."

Chapter 19

They walked farther along the path, which was just wide enough for two to walk together. Jill and Nikolos led, the passengers followed, and Damia and Rook watched their backs. A half hour later, the path began to widen, growing to perhaps twenty feet wide and continuing for twice that far before narrowing again.

"Oh!" Zarah cried out as soon as she stepped into the wider part. Her eyes squeezed shut, her mouth twisted into a grimace, and her hand went to her stomach. She wobbled and reached out one arm blindly.

Alaric touched her elbow to steady her. "Are you all right?"

"Something is wrong here. Something is here that should not be." Zarah's voice sounded far away.

Alaric could almost feel Zarah's stomach twisting, almost feel the pounding in her temples. "I don't see anything dangerous. I don't see anything different at all."

"It screams in my head. It grinds all sound to silence. Get me out of here. Please, get me out of here!" Zarah cried.

"What is it?" Alaric looked around again, trying to find the source of Zarah's fear and pain. "What's different?"

"Can we keep moving?" Damia said, "There's nothing different here."

"This is different." Professor Lamarca knelt and pointed out a thin brown vine trailing along the path.

"A vine?" Damia said. "They're everywhere. And this one at least isn't trying to kill us."

"Look closely," Lamarca said. "It's different."

Alaric took a good look at the thin, gray-brown vine. "It's hard and prickly, like it would grow thorns if it were bigger. And it's the wrong shade of brown. I see it."

"Blades out," the captain said. "Eyes open. Keep moving." She drew her machete. Rook, Nikolos, and Damia followed suit.

Zarah forced herself forward. She kept her eyes focused on the path in front of her, struggling with every step.

Alaric kept pace with her. "Do you think the blades will help?"

Zarah bit her lip. "I don't know."

"Isn't the island guiding you?"

"Not anymore." Zarah's steps and speech grew faster. "I can't hear the Flower. For the first time in weeks, I can't hear the World Flower."

"Isn't that a relief?" Alaric asked. "You have your mind to yourself."

"It should be. It really should be," Zarah said. "Please, hurry."

"There are more of these strange vines," Lamarca said, "They're getting bigger. These have thorns. Oh! I know what's different."

"What?" Jill asked.

"Everything else here is fresh and new green life, like an endless springtime. These are old, hardened, like plants that are going into winter. I wonder why," Lamarca said.

Damia pointed with her machete. "Maybe we can ask them."

Two skeletal forms, like two cruel mockeries of men, unwound themselves from a tangle of growth. Writhing vines wrapped themselves into limbs and knots. Empty holes raged where their eyes should have been. At the end of each arm-like branch was a five-fingered knot with thorns as long as knives.

Alaric knew them from the vision. "The thorn men."

"Run." Zarah's voice rose from a whisper to a shout. "Run! We've got to run!"

"No," Nikolos said. "We fight."

Nikolos and Damia stood firm, blades raised. With the same motion, they reached for the small metal shields they wore on their scabbards. The bucklers were nine inches across and shaped like domes. Nikolos and Damia gripped them like metal fists, ready to strike or defend.

"I could destroy these two myself," Damia said. "I will not run."

"Looks like they heard you," Rook said.

The two creatures rushed forward, their movements swift but jerky, like they were not used to their man-like forms. They rushed toward the front of the group, their thorn-claws ready to strike.

Jill shouldered past Alaric and met the foremost thorn man head on. It swung its five-thorned claw in a wide arc. She met the attack with a sweeping cut. The machete bit deep into the thick, thorny vine. Milky white sap poured from the cut, and the thorn claw flopped backward, useless. She laughed as she brought her machete back down on the creature's neck. "I guess you were right about that song, kid."

Near the trunk of the great tree, more forms emerged from the vines. Twisted knots burst open like tumors, releasing the terrors within.

"I hope their sap is not corrosive." Maxime ducked back to the edge of the path, as far as he could get from the thorn men. "If it is, I shudder to think what will happen the next time we face them, when all our blades are rust."

Damia rushed at the second thorn man. She slammed her buckler where a person's face would be. It rocked back and nearly tumbled of the edge. Damia slashed down with her machete, severing its left branch at the shoulder. The creature flowed and writhed downward to slash at her upper leg. She just got the buckler down in time. The thorns shrieked against the metal, leaving deep grooves in the steel shield.

She started to punch out, but stopped. Alaric remembered the sword she wore, with its d-shaped handguard. She could have safely driven that right into the thorn man. But the machete had no hand protection at all. If she tried, she'd only break her fingers. Damia wasted half a second fighting her instincts. She quickly recovered and slashed down at the viny neck.

The thorn man flowed out of reach and rushed at Alaric. He drew the only weapon he had: a simple pocketknife. Its little blade was more suited for camping than fighting.

"Quickly!" The captain shouted. "They're trying to cut off our escape!"

Down the path, Nikolos kept two thorn men at bay with his machete and buckler. Rook watched his back to make sure nothing came around behind him. With each swing, bits of thorn wood flew into the air with a spray of milky sap. Neither could close with him, and in time he would surely destroy them both. If their sap didn't melt his blade first.

Zarah tugged on Alaric's shirt. "Hurry! We've got to go!"

"Then go," Alaric said. "Get to safety. I'll try to hold these things back."

Jill drove her machete into the thorn man again. "Stay down, drown you!"

Three more creatures rushed toward them. Jill and Damia stepped into their path, blades slashing. They held two of the creatures up, but the third slipped between them and rushed toward Alaric.

"Another one?" Alaric glanced over his shoulder. "It's Zarah. Zarah! Captain! They're not after us! They're after her!"

"Zarah?" the captain said. "Why are they after her?"

"I thought the island wanted her here!" Damia said.

"These things don't!" Alaric said.

"Hurry then! Go with her!" Jill swung a two-handed cut across a thorn man's trunk. White sap spilled down onto the path and dripped down to the ground far below.

Jill ran after the one that passed her earlier, slashing at it from behind. She hacked it in half, then she kicked its top half off the path. "We'll hold the line until you're clear."

Zarah ran. Alaric stayed close to her. He could hear Maxime's hard breathing behind him and Lamarca's rustling robes.

He glanced over his shoulder and saw Nikolos slice one of the thorn men in half. Damia swept another one's head off, but it kept fighting, swinging wildly. He looked over and saw thorn men clinging to the underside of the pathway, trying to surround them.

"Behind you!" Alaric shouted. "They're coming from underneath!"

The first of the thorn men sprang up from under the path. The captain cut it down and kicked it off the side. "Come on!"

Rook hacked at a thorn man as it pulled itself onto the path. Each hit left deep gashes in the gray-brown wood. As soon as he finished the creature, another took its place.

Jill sliced the branch off another thorn man just before it cut Rook down. Damia followed. Then four more creatures climbed up onto the path, cutting off their escape.

Damia slashed at them from behind while Jill cut them from the front. Nikolos held the rear guard. He swung his machete in wide arcs. The circular motions kept the thorn men at a distance and sliced parts off of those that drew too close. He kept his dagger in his other hand, ready to block or stab at anything that passed the slashing wall of his machete.

Damia held a buckler in her left hand. The small steel shield was just thick enough to stop the thorns. She punched out with the buckler, knocking a thorn man off balance. Then she brought the machete down in an overhand slice. Her entire body powered the attack, from her feet all the way through her body to her arm. She almost launched herself off the ground as she struck. The machete sliced the thorn man in half. One half fell from the path while the other toppled over.

The next thorn man gave her no rest. It leapt at her, slashing like a feral cat. Damia retreated, blocking with both shield and machete. She moved so quickly that Alaric's eyes could scarcely follow. But the force of the thorn man's blows drove her back to the edge of the path.

Jill couldn't help her. She was fighting two thorn men herself.

"Rook!" Alaric called out. "Help Damia!" He hoped Rook was a better fighter than Nikolos had let on.

Rook turned and hurried back down.

But before he could get to her, Damia had helped herself. She ducked and tripped the thorn man. It stumbled, off-balance. A punch from the buckler sent it tumbling off the path.

Their numbers seemed endless. The bright green of the path was slick and white with spilled sap. And they kept coming.

Three thorn men blocked the path forward, and Nikolos held four at bay by himself. But more crawled onto the pathway, pressing in on them on every side.

Alaric turned to Zarah. "There are too many. We can't keep this up. Maybe we can cut a path through and you can escape."

"With that knife?" Zarah asked. "I could do more good just shoving them off the side."

Alaric turned to the scholars. "Any ideas?"

"Hmm," Lamarca said. "I've noticed that the creatures are always touching the vines. Sometimes they're on smallest of the vines, sometimes the larger ones. But always something. They don't exist on the pure green."

"Unfortunately, the vines seem to be everywhere," Maxime said.

Alaric took a quick breath and calmed himself. He needed to see beyond the battle, beyond the scholars' words and the fear of death. "There! That branch, on the canopy side. Do you see any thorns?"

"No. None of them have come within five feet of it," Lamarca said.

"That's our way out," Alaric said. "It cuts across to the canopy, then up to a different section of the path. If it works, we'll be safe there."

Maxime made a choking sound. "That's an awfully small branch."

"I've climbed smaller things," Alaric said, "but you should be careful. Zarah, make for that branch." He raised his voice. "Cover us! We've found a way out!"

"Form up!" Jill shouted the order, then swung her sword in a wide, sweeping cut. She drew a line of sap across one thorny trunk. The creature drew back.

Nikolos retreated, still swinging his sword widely. Rook and Damia joined him. The sailors formed a half-circle. Their blades and faces were white with sap, their clothes torn, their breath ragged.

"There are too many of them," Nikolos said. "Even I can't keep this up forever."

"Alaric found a way out. We'll buy him time." The captain's hands were shaking, but she held tight to her blade.

Alaric climbed onto the branch and offered his hand to Zarah. "Come on." She stepped wrong, and the branch bent beneath her. Alaric grabbed her arm. She was heavy, but strong. He didn't have to hold her up, just steady her. "You're going to have to trust me."

Zarah nodded. She let him lead her up the branch.

The sounds of the battle raged behind him, but Alaric didn't dare look back. "You're doing great, and not a thorn in sight. We'll have to climb from here."

Zarah followed, keeping her eyes on the climb.

When Alaric reached the top, he grabbed Zarah's arm and pulled her up behind him. "Are you all right?"

"I can hear it again," Zarah whispered. "I can hear the World Flower again. I can't believe that's a good thing."

"Come on!" Alaric shouted down. "It's safe."

Lamarca made the climb with a little help. Maxime barely made it.

"We're clear!" Alaric shouted. The sailors disengaged with the creatures one at a time. First Rook, then Damia, hurried to the branch. After some argument, Jill ran for safety. Nikolos Mordos was the last to run. He held the thorn men off until everyone else was safe.

Slowly, steadily, and carefully, they made their way to where Zarah stood. The thorn men did not follow.

"Are we safe here?" Jill asked. She kept her machete pointed at the path behind them. Alaric looked at the blade. It hadn't melted away. That was something to be thankful for.

"I hear the voice of the World Flower again." Zarah's eyes had lost their focus once more, but the fear had left her voice.

Jill scowled. "That's not an answer, Miss Remei."

"I don't see any more of those vines," Lamarca said. "I think we're beyond their reach for now."

"That's closer to an answer," the captain said. "Miss Remei, are we safe here?"

"I am safe here," Zarah said. "The thorn men cannot come here. They will not go where the sunlight filters through the flowers and the leaves are soft and green. But don't think that you are safe."

"We didn't come here to be safe." Nikolos looked like a monster himself. Milky sap spattered his clothes and hair, marked here and there with little splashes of red. Sweat pressed his thick black hair to his skin. "We came here for the treasure. We know it's real now. 'Search the dark heart where the thorn men are born.'"

Damia laughed. "I have to admit, I wasn't sure we'd find it before. This is the greatest treasure in the world, and we're going to claim it."

"You don't think that could be the place, do you?" Rook asked. "It looked like the thorn men were being born there. Maybe it was the dark heart?"

"Those vines were too exposed to hide a treasure," Nikolos said. "But I'm sure it's close at hand."

"We've got one sure mission: to get Miss Remei to her flower," Jill said. "I want that treasure as much as anybody, but I don't want to die for it." The captain wiped her machete on the soft moss of the path. "At least this sap couldn't melt steel."

"We were lucky to find that path this time," Alaric said. "If we have to face those things again, we might not be lucky. We'll need a plan."

Lamarca shook her head. "Unless I can figure out what they are and why they're attacking, I can't plan. Just look for a path with none of their vines and try to escape again."

"That's not a plan," Alaric said. "That's blind hope."

"I know. It's all I have right now."

Maxime shook his head. "That's all any of us have. That's the story of this journey."

Chapter 20

Rook stared back down the path. "Are you sure those things can't leave their vines?" The thorn men stared hatefully. They slashed uselessly with their thorn-claws, and the hollows where their eyes should have been pulsed with rage.

"If they could, we'd be dead right now," Jill said. "Rest while you can. I'm sure there's more trouble ahead."

Nikolos wiped milky sap from the blade of his machete. "We'll be ready."

Damia tested her blade to make sure it was still sharp. "We can't stay here forever, and those brown vines are everywhere."

Alaric looked around the lush area where they stood safe—for now. Branches from the great tree at the center of the tower had woven together to form a platform below and a shelter above. Lush leaves shaded them from the hot afternoon sun. The air smelled fresh and somehow…green. He wanted to lie down and sleep, but he wondered if he'd ever wake up, or want to.

"Let's go," Jill said. "If we stay here too long, we'll get stiff and sore, and we'll lose our nerve. We can't go back safely. The only way out is up. The sooner we reach the top, the sooner we'll be safe."

Alaric knew she was right, but he didn't have to like it.

"As I said, we didn't come here to be safe," Nikolos said.

"The sooner we reach the top, the sooner we find the treasure," Damia said, "in the place where the thorn men are born."

"I know the song," the captain said. "'The Ballad of Captain Valens' has guided us this far."

"Zarah has guided us this far," Alaric said.

"Then guide us onward." Jill said. "We're going now." They left the platform in silence, as if even Nikolos and Damia felt its peaceful pull. The path flexed under their feet with every step. Usually, that would be unnerving, but now it meant it was still new and green.

"I don't see any vines on the path," Alaric said.

Zarah pointed to the great tree that supported the entire tower. Its trunk had hardened to a thorny gray. Even the canopy of leaves grew darker.

"Oh," Alaric whispered. "We're not safe."

Zarah shook her head.

"So now you're as much a target as we are," Alaric said.

"I knew I'd have to face the thorn men," Zarah said.

"But?" Alaric asked. "I know that's not the end of that sentence."

Zarah sighed. "I don't know if I'm more afraid of failing or succeeding. I want to cure the plague. I just don't know what will happen to me."

"If we fail, we die," Alaric said.

"I was going to die someday anyway," Zarah said. "At least I'd die me. If I succeed, will I even know? Will there be anything left of me to celebrate?"

"Oh." Alaric walked beside her in silence for a while. The path stayed green and soft, but the tree grew grayer and thornier. "It's not fair."

"Fair?"

Alaric laughed bitterly. "I know nothing is fair. Fair is a lie people tell themselves to feel better when they lose, or when they win without deserving to."

Zarah chuckled softly. "You haven't completely left the docks behind."

"Guilty," Alaric said. "Still, this all seems worse. More unfair. Actually unfair. The crew chose this. The scholars chose this. I chose this. The depths know I fought for this."

"You didn't have many options," Zarah said, "that doesn't seem fair to me."

"It isn't. But I chose this. I fought for this. You were dragged into this by the World Flower. The rest of us came willingly. We all had our reasons. Some were more desperate than others. But the professors were already working on a cure. The crew wants the treasure. And I want…. You know what I want."

"The university," Zarah said, "because you have to earn it. Because no one can fake or buy a degree."

"But you're innocent in all this," Alaric said. "You were dragged into this situation by some divine power."

"I wasn't," Zarah said quietly.

"What?"

Zarah bit her lip. "I chose all of this. The plants always talked to me, but they never demanded much. One day, my neighbor caught a fever. I asked the plants to show me how to make a cure, and they did. So, when the news of the plague came, I asked them to help me cure that."

"You asked the plants to cure the plague?" Alaric asked. "What did they say?"

"They brought me to a place where I could communicate with the World Flower. The divine is real. I've seen it, talked with it."

"What did it say?"

"The World Flower warned me that it wouldn't be simple or easy. It would take everything I am. Even if I survived, I wouldn't be the same. I said I'd do it. Even if I die, my friends and family will live."

"Zarah—"

"I'm no victim. No matter what happens, this is my choice. Just like your fate is yours." Zarah looked around her and shivered. "The

World Flower's call is so powerful on this island. It almost swallowed me up. Now I can hardly hear it, and that scares me."

"It scares me too," Alaric said. "I think it scares us all."

"Even the wolves?" Zarah asked.

Alaric glanced back at Nikolos and Damia. "Even wolves get scared. That's when they're most likely to bite."

Zarah forced a smile. "One more thing to be scared of."

"Hey, what's that?" Damia said. "Is that a sword?"

Alaric looked and saw a rusted bar of metal poking out of the tree's trunk. "How can you tell?"

"It has the same d-guard as my saber," Damia said. "Look at the shape. Even though it's rusted, there's only one thing it could be."

"Even if it isn't a sword, it's metal," Nikolos said. "It didn't come from this island."

"We're not the first ones here." Alaric felt a thrill of possibility and chill of danger at once. "If that was Captain Valens's sword, then the stories are true. The treasure is here."

Damia walked around to get a different angle. "Look from here. There's a gemstone at the very end of the pommel. This was definitely a rich man's sword." A wolf's smile crossed her face. The light that filled her eyes was not joy but hunger.

Alaric looked at Nikolos and Damia. "Hope and hunger are a dangerous combination," he whispered to Zarah.

Zarah leaned close and whispered back, "The hope of wolves is terror to lambs."

One look at Zarah's face told him they were thinking the same thing: while the treasure was merely possible, Nikolos and Damia were dangerous and unpredictable, but now it's real.

"Anyone standing between them and the treasure is a dead man walking," Zarah said. "Are you sure you don't want to split up?"

"Until we figure out how to deal with the thorn men, we have to take our chances," Alaric whispered. "Nikolos and Damia may kill us in the end, but without them, we won't make it that far."

Chapter 21

"All right, you have your evidence." Captain Jill Crimson pointed at the rusted, jeweled sword sticking out of the great tree's trunk. "The treasure's on this island, but it isn't here, so keep moving."

Nikolos and Damia stalked up the path with renewed energy, fired up from the proof they'd found.

The captain pressed onward, tired but professional, unwilling to show weakness.

The others trudged up the path two abreast, keeping a few feet between them and the edge. The thorn men's milky sap clung to everything, drying on their clothes and hair. Its sour-sweet smell drowned the freshness of the leaves and the perfume of the flowers. Legs burned, backs ached, and thorn-wounds throbbed.

Alaric nodded and grunted, too ragged and exhausted from the last two attacks to notice. The burning in his legs had settled into a grinding ache, settled so deep he could barely feel it. He could scarcely remember ever not feeling draining, dreary pain.

"Come on, boy," Nikolos said. "Why so slow? We just found proof that the treasure is real. This is what you want, isn't it?"

Alaric nodded, but he couldn't bring himself to say yes.

"He'll perk up when he sees the gems," Damia said. "Keep up, kid, or we'll leave you behind."

"You may leave us all behind," Maxime said. "We're all wearing bandages. Some are blood soaked. We barely removed half the sap from their skin and clothes. The treasure brightened your steps, but how long will that last?"

"Long enough," Damia said.

"We're in trouble if they attack again," Alaric whispered.

"When they attack again," Zarah replied.

Nikolos stared at the massive tree trunk. "Do you see the discoloration? It gets darker as we go. Look, there. Up and around, in the direction of the path. It gets darker still."

Damia leaned close and looked where he was pointing. "I see it! The edges of a hollow, or a rot-out."

"That is where the thorn men are born," Nikolos said.

"Then we're close." Damia's smile brought a chill to Alaric's spine. "We're close to the treasure. And we've left our weakest members behind. We have a chance now to take what's ours. I say we press on."

"Aye," Nikolos said, "press on."

The captain frowned. "We'll not stay here long. Give Zarah a moment. And don't forget her mission. Don't forget what brought us here."

Nikolos stared at his sister. "I remember why we're here. Do you?"

"It's on our way to the World Flower," Jill said. "We'll see what's there. If we can get the treasure, we will." She looked back at where Maxime and Lamarca lay. "But I'm not throwing our lives away."

"We'll have to fight either way," Nikolos said. "When the time comes, I'll fight to claim what's ours. I'll take that risk. We're closer to real wealth than we've ever been. I can see it."

"We are close to the World Flower." Zarah sounded far away again, not like herself at all. "I hear it calling, even through the thorns. Soon we will reach it. Soon."

"We'll make that decision when we get there." The captain stared at the path ahead. "I want that treasure as much as you do, little brother, but I won't see you killed for it. You can't spend a copper farthing if you're dead, much less a king's ransom. And I need my brother more than I need a box of gems."

Nikolos frowned. "Very well. Lead on."

Fear and suspicion marked each step they took. Every blade was ready. Every set of eyes darted from high to low, searching for any little grey-brown vine. Alaric missed having Professor Lamarca there to tell him about the plants. He missed both of the scholars. He hoped they were alive, but he couldn't spare more thoughts than that.

With each step, the platform gave just a little under Alaric's feet. He'd grown accustomed to it over the climb. Soon it gave less. Soon it felt harder, more solid. Suddenly, it did not give at all.

"Look out!" Alaric shouted.

Four thorny forms dropped from above. Six more crawled onto the path from below.

Nikolos gave an overhand slice, splitting a thorn man, then kicked it off the platform. It fell, trailing pale sap behind.

Jill swung high, catching a thorn man mid-trunk. The creature's momentum carried it through her blade, cutting it in half. Its bottom half fell into the darkness below. But its top half clung to a vine. It lashed out, five thorns slashing wildly. Another hit from the captain sent it spinning, still holding the vine. She took that moment's opening to slice through the vine. The creature tumbled into the darkness below.

"Send them off the sides!" She called out. "We can cut them into pieces, but the pieces will keep fighting."

Damia faked a high attack. Then she reversed her swing and hacked into a thorn man's leg. She punched out with her buckler, and the creature tumbled off the side.

Rook struggled to hold his own against a single thorn man. He found himself on the defensive, desperately blocking every blow.

Alaric instinctively reached for his ash-and-pepper packets but stopped himself. They'd do nothing against a creature with no eyes, no mouth, and no nose. Instead, he drew his knife. He lunged and drove it into thorn man's knotty body. Then he used the knife as a handle to wrench the wretched monster off the side. It fell into the depths, taking his knife with it.

"Thanks!" Rook said. "It looks like I owe you my life."

"I don't need your life. What would I do with your life?" Alaric smiled. "But you do owe me a knife."

"Keep moving!" Jill said. "No telling how many of them there are. They might keep coming forever."

With each opening they pressed forward. But every ten feet they faced another wave of thorn men. Tired and wounded as they were, they could barely fight the creatures. But the decision to knock them off the side rather than to try to destroy them proved wise. And they slowly progressed up the path.

Nikolos pointed ahead at a gaping hole in the trunk. "Look! The dark heart where the thorn men are born."

Alaric had never thought of what a festering wound would look like on a tree. But he knew now.

"Keep fighting," the captain said. "Keep going. The attacks will only get worse. We have to pass that pit. If that's where they are born, there's no telling what they'll do to defend it. And drown it all, the path's getting wider. We'll face more of them before we face fewer."

Rook cried out as a thorn man's claws raked across his forearm. His machete went spinning across the ground. He staggered back, and the thorn man loomed large. The captain lunged to his rescue. She slashed down at the creature and drove it back over the edge.

"There are too many of them!" Jill shouted, "Look out!"

A thorn man pushed past her and rushed toward Zarah. Alaric braced himself and stepped in front of her. Before he could act, Maxime and Lamarca shoved past him and spread their robes wide.

"Get her to safety!" Lamarca called out, "She has to – ugh!"

The thorn man drove its claws into her gut. Then slammed Maxime into the hard side of the path. Both scholars fell, wounded unconscious, to the ground.

"Zarah! Zarah, focus," Alaric said. "Listen to my voice. If you can hear the World Flower, talk to it. I can't see any path here, but there has to be one. There has to be some way out."

Zarah closed her eyes and drew in a deep breath. When she opened them again, they almost seemed to glow. "There." She pointed to a thin line of branches leading upward. They were far too small to walk on, just thick enough hold a man's weight. "If we climb across those, we can escape."

Damia cried out and shoved one of the creatures off the edge. His thorn fingers pulled out of her shoulder with a cruel wet sound. Her left arm hung limp. Jill drove another thorn man off the side of the path. For a moment, there was an opening.

"Come on!" Alaric ran toward the branches, pulling Zarah with him. She climbed on first and shimmied up and across the branch. Alaric followed.

Rook collected his machete, awkwardly slid it into its sheath, and hurried after them.

"Damia, you're next," Jill said. "Nikolos and I will hold the line."

Damia sheathed her blade and followed after. Her left arm still clung to the buckler, but she couldn't move it. The best she could do was tuck it against her chest as she climbed.

"You go on," Nikolos said. "I'll follow." He swept his machete in wide arcs, splitting vines in sprays of milk-white sap. "Don't argue. Just hurry." He punched a thorn man in the face. It staggered back but did not fall.

The captain sheathed her blade and scrambled onto the branch, making way for her brother.

Nikolos slashed out with his blade one last time, then ran and jumped for the branch. He let his buckler fall and grabbed hold with his left hand, keeping his machete in his right.

The thorn men stood at the base of the branch, clacking their thorns together. They moaned and wailed hungrily, but they did not follow.

Zarah followed the path of the branch upward to another rounded, freestanding clearing. This platform was half-knotted with thorn vines. Only a small section was safe from the thorn men.

Alaric helped Rook off the vine, then turned to aid Damia.

"I don't want your help, kid," she said.

"You're injured," Alaric said. "By the depths! Take my hand."

"Fine." Damia took his hand and let him pull her to safety, but she scowled and glared at him the whole time.

"It doesn't mean you're weak," Alaric said. "You could probably still beat me one-handed."

"No doubt about it," Damia said. The instant her feet touched solid ground, she drew her machete.

Jill and Nikolos dropped easily from the branch, then drew their blades as well.

Jill leaned over, hands on her knees, catching her breath. "A brave thing those scholars did. Braver than any swordsman I've seen."

Nikolos frowned but nodded. "It was indeed."

"So, what are we going to do about them?" Rook asked. The two scholars lay on the path behind them, their robes flat and dark against the green. "We can't just leave them here."

"We have to," the captain said. "If we go back in there and try to drag them out, the thorns will get us."

"But we can't just leave them to die!" Rook said.

"If Zarah reaches the World Flower, she can put some of this right," Alaric said. "I think. I hope."

"Zarah?" Jill asked.

"The World Flower told me that I had to heal it before it could heal the plague. I think I have to heal the island too. Maybe that will wake them."

"That's a big maybe," Rook said, "but we can't do anything for them now but hope."

Jill turned to Damia. "Can you fight? You can barely climb."

"I've got one good hand," Damia said through gritted teeth. "That's all I need."

"Look." Rook's face grew ashy, and his voice trembled. "Look, there. It's the heart."

Nikolos's face lit up with a predatory joy. "The heart! The treasure is inside. Our future is inside. If we claim it, we are not just rich. We are legends."

A gaping hole the size of the counting house's doors had rotted out of the tree. Thorny gray vines as thick as a man's thigh grew from the darkness of the heart. They twisted out around the trunk, choking the branches. From them, all the smaller vines and thorns grew.

Dozens of thorn men clung to the twisting vines. More climbed out of the darkness to join them. And every one kept its eyeless gaze fixed on Zarah Remei.

"I hate to argue with the first mate," Rook said, "but we aren't legends. We aren't rich. We're dead. We have come all this way, and now we are dead."

"Rook Corbin, don't you lose hope on me." There was an unusual tremble in the Jill's voice.

Rook shook his head. "Captain, it was an honor. Alaric, it was good to meet you. Zarah, I'm sorry. I'm truly sorry. I don't think we can save you now."

Chapter 22

Alaric stared into the dark heart, the place where the thorn men are born, the source of the rot within the sacred island. Gray-brown vines as thick as his waist wound out from the center, their thorns as long as daggers. They split and twisted into smaller and smaller vines, infiltrating the green. The fresh scent of the leaves could not reach the dark heart. Here, it was as dry and empty as snowless winter.

Dozens of thorn men clung to the twisting vines. Dozens of eyeless faces stared at Zarah. Dozens of thorny hands twitched.

Damia shifted her feet and raised her machete. "What are they waiting for? Why don't they attack? Why aren't they doing anything?"

A smile crossed the captain's face. "They're defending the nest. This could be the opportunity we need. We can get away. We can get Zarah to the flower and stop the plague."

Zarah's face turned pale, and her lips took on a blue tint. She wobbled on her feet, and finally sank to one knee. "It's me. Their purpose is to protect their home, but they really want me dead. They're struggling. They're trying to decide whether to leave the dark heart and come after me."

Alaric pulled Zarah to her feet. "Let's get out of here before they make up their mind."

"And leave the treasure behind?" Damia waved her blade in the direction of her limp and useless left arm. "I didn't suffer this for nothing. I didn't fight and bleed to just give up. I don't know if this will heal right. My left arm may never work again. I demand repayment! I demand revenge! I will not go home one-armed and empty-handed."

"If you try to go in there, none of us will go home at all," Alaric said. "We'll all die here."

Nikolos pointed at the tree. "It looks like they've made up their minds." Thorn men slowly dragged themselves away from the entrance. The creatures stalked along the thorn vines toward them. "We're in for a fight. We may as well take the prize."

"How?" Alaric asked. "There are too many of them for us to fight, even if we all had weapons. Far too many."

"They are not after us," Nikolos said. "They do not care about us. They want Zarah. We tell her to run. We send them after her. And then we pierce the heart and take the treasure."

"The depths you will!" Alaric said. "They'll kill her!"

"Mr. Mordos...." Zarah struggled to speak, as if fog had descended upon her mind. Each word came haltingly, but with such force of emotion that no one interrupted. "Remember why I'm here. There's a plague. Tens of thousands will die. Maybe hundreds of thousands will die. Millions will get sick. I can stop that suffering. But I have to get to the World Flower."

Nikolos said. "I don't care about strangers in a distant land."

"The plague will reach Solok in time," Alaric said, "and Thervingi. Everyone we know will suffer."

"I don't care about my homeland." Nikolos's face twisted into a cold scowl. "No one there ever gave me anything but trouble. I learned early that I would have nothing but what I take for myself. And I will take this treasure."

Alaric heard his own words in Nikolos's mouth, and he did not like the sound of them.

"I wasn't given a life either," Alaric said. "You know that. I had to struggle for everything. I work for every meal."

"Then you understand! Why should we sacrifice our future for theirs when they gave us nothing? What do we owe them?"

"What about Zarah?" Alaric asked. "She's one of us. We owe her loyalty."

"She's not one of us," Nikolos said. "Her scholar friends paid us a fee. I'll refund it from my share of the treasure. But we are taking it."

The captain broke her silence. "No. The answer is no. This is not just treason, it's madness. We signed a contract. We made a deal. We gave our word."

"We will never need another contract once we have this treasure." Nikolos's face went from pale to red. "We'll never need to kiss another ring or sail the gray or learn another endless book of trade regulations again. When we have this treasure, we'll be rich enough to make our own rules. And the depths take anyone who dares cross us!"

"I gave my word," Jill said. "The crew agreed with me to take this job. You agreed to take this job. That means something. My word means something."

"Your word means throwing away our chance at greatness? Our chance at true freedom? Our chance to stop living in fear?" Nikolos's breathing grew heavy. He seemed to grow even bigger as his rage built. "I am your brother. We are family. Does your word mean more than your own blood?"

The captain stared down her brother. "We don't know what's in there, but we know what's surrounding it. I see more thorn men than we could ever beat. You think they'll all go after Zarah? How many do you think it will take to kill one little girl? How many will stay behind to slaughter us?"

"You're afraid. You would let our future slip away because you're afraid? Stop protecting me! Stop stranding me in mediocrity. Stop chaining me to this hateful fate because you're scared." Nikolos stepped towards his sister, his blade still in his hand.

Rook stepped between them, his hand reaching for his machete. "You can't talk to the captain like that."

Nikolos brought his blade down on the old sailor's shoulder, driving him to the ground. Rook lay there, gasping for breath, his eyes wide in shock.

The captain threw her blade down and shoved Nikolos. "What in the depths are you doing?"

Nikolos caught the shove and flung his sister aside. The throw was so fast Alaric almost didn't see it.

The captain flew off the platform with a cry of surprise.

Alaric didn't know whether the first mate moved out of rage or instinct. Maybe Nikolos didn't know. But no matter his motives, Jill vanished into the darkness below.

Nikolos stared over the edge. He stood frozen in place, as if he was trying to figure out what happened to his sister. As if he was trying to figure out whether he'd really thrown her over the edge.

Then he turned to face Alaric. His rage had turned cold, and his face was as pale as ice. "It comes down to this, boy. You can stand with us, or you can fall with them. But we will take the treasure, whatever the cost to this girl. Or you."

"Nikolos, what did you do?" Alaric whispered.

"It's time to choose," Nikolos said quietly.

Rook lay face down, struggling for air. His body was so broken. There was no human way to save him. The captain was gone, swallowed up by the darkness below.

Alaric stepped to his left, trying to block Nikolos's view of Zarah.

"The captain." Alaric's voice caught in his throat. The voice in the back of his mind told him to stop. The voice that spun the truth, that kept him alive in Port Theron, stuttered and screamed for him to shut up. But the words would not stop. "Your sister. You…your sister…."

"Choose!" Nikolos shouted. "The treasure is here. The treasure you came for is here. Zarah Remei is going to die. We are going to get the treasure. Who do you stand with? Which do you choose, wealth or poverty? Life or death?" With each word, Nikolos stepped closer. "Help us or die with her. Choose!"

"Nikolos, why?" Alaric asked.

"Choose! Now!" The first mate's rage rose again, coloring his pale face red.

Damia stood beside him silently, eyes calm, her blade in her hand. "Choose, boy, or we choose for you."

Alaric threw the packet of ash and dried pepper into Nikolos's face. The packet burst into a gray-red cloud. Nikolos jolted back, coughing and spitting. "Run!" Alaric didn't wait to look. He ran after Zarah.

The path felt first hard, then yielding under Alaric's feet. This close to the top, the World Flower and the thorn men battled for control of the path. He didn't have to look down to see the thorns. He didn't have time to look around and see what was waiting for them.

A roar rose behind Alaric, followed by the wet sound of a machete hacking through vines. "Thorn men!" Two landed on the path ahead of him. Their eyeless faces turned toward Zarah.

"This way!" Zarah grabbed Alaric's hand and pulled him off the side of the path. They fell just a few feet and landed on interlocking branches. "The thorn men corrupted the path, but the Flower grew a way around."

They scrambled across the narrow pathway until it rejoined the main path. Alaric glanced behind him and saw Nikolos cut the last of the thorn men down. "They're gaining on us! We've lost our lead!"

"It doesn't matter! We're close!"

"You said that before." Alaric's lungs burned, and his head felt weak and dizzy. His feet began to stumble. "I've been running too long. I don't know if I can do this."

"You can," Zarah said. "You've already done something much harder. Nikolos and Damia chose a life of greed. You chose honesty and goodness. You gave up a dream to help me and help a bunch of folks you never met. I won't forget that. You wonder how I'll remember you? That's how."

"That's if either of us gets out of this alive." They were not the words Alaric had wanted to say. "No, sorry. I mean, thank you. Even if we die, that means a lot."

"We're not dead yet—look out!" Zarah pulled Alaric out of the way as a vine slashed out. They rolled to the side and clung to the narrow path. Another vine whipped down, dragging its thorns across the leafy path, trying to cut it out of the sky. Alaric struggled to get his feet under him. As Nikolos's footsteps thundered closer, another vine rose up to strike.

Suddenly, Nikolos cried out. A bright green vine wrapped around his arm, and another one around his thigh. Damia ran up and slashed through the vines, but more came.

The thorn vine slashed out against the green vines. The green vines wrapped and grew around the thorns, slowing them. Milky white sap and thick clear sap dripped onto the path.

"Stay clear of that!" Alaric said. "That clear sap ate through a machete blade."

Zarah grabbed his hand and pulled him forward. A writhing mass of vines blocked the way forward. Thorns and tendrils twisted together. White and clear sap dripped onto the path below.

"We can't go through there!" Alaric said.

"Trust me." Zarah crawled into the mass of vines.

Alaric glanced behind him. Nikolos and Damia pulled free of the vines. Damia's blade was melting away, but she hacked with what remained, cutting through green and gray alike.

"Looks like I don't have much choice," Alaric followed Zarah through the tangle of vines. The thorns twitched and jerked, but the green held them just out of reach. The brown-gray vine grappled and twisted until its thorns gashed into the green. A heavy drop of clear, thick sap dropped onto Alaric's face. He winced and cried out but felt no pain. "It didn't burn me."

"You're not made of steel," Zarah called over her shoulder.

"It looks like they want you to get through. But why are the vines letting me through?"

"Maybe you earned the World Flower's respect when you stood up to Nikolos. Maybe it thinks you're useful for now. Don't get too used to it."

"I won't. I'm sure it will tire of me soon enough," Alaric said.

"It's staying out of my head, too," Zarah said. "Letting me make my own choices. Maybe it's starting to trust us."

They emerged from the tangle of vines and dragged themselves to their feet. Alaric bent over for a moment to catch his breath. "Do you think they could get through that?"

They stood on a small platform, no more than a dozen feet across. The gray-brown vines only reached the very edges. The thorn men glared from just out of reach.

"They're coming!" Zarah pointed back along the path.

Alaric heard a roaring and a shrieking. He saw vines twisting and falling before Nikolos's and Damia's blades.

Alaric backed away to the edge of the platform, keeping himself between them and Zarah. By the time they reached the platform, Damia's machete was corroded away to little more than a handle. She tossed it to the ground and drew her dagger. "And now you're both going to die." Her eyes flared wide and wild with anger. But they paled before the rage on Nikolos's face.

Nikolos stalked slowly across the platform. "We have one machete left. One knife. And no chance to get the treasure. Because of you." He paced side to side, not even closing with them. His breathing slowed. His rage congealed into malice, like poison distilled, concentrated, thickening as it cooled. His scowl turned to the cruelest smile Alaric had ever seen. "We're stranded in this grave of thorns and flowers because of you. My sister is dead because of you!"

"You threw Jill off the platform!" Zarah said. "That's your fault. You did that. Own up to what you did!"

"Shut up, girl!" Rage burst through the savage calm, but Nikolos pushed it back down. He paced back and forth, growing ever closer. "That was not my fault."

Alaric glanced around him, trying to find some way to escape. "Zarah, is there a way out?"

She closed her eyes and took a deep breath. "Behind us. Run, then jump."

"It was your fault," Alaric spoke loudly, hoping to distract from their whispering. "You cut down your crewmate with no just cause. You threw your sister to her death. You did that. Not me. Not Rook Corbin, not Zarah, and not the captain. You did that."

"Shut up! Shut up, drown you!" Nikolos bellowed the words, his face red, his eyes shut with rage. "Shut up! That was not my fault!"

"Now!" Alaric said. Zarah turned and ran, and Alaric followed. He jumped when she jumped, not knowing where they were going to land. They made it across a small gap and up a thin branch.

Nikolos rushed the edge of the platform and lashed out with the machete, roaring and cursing their names. The branch shook, but Alaric and Zarah kept hold.

"Where to now?" Alaric asked.

"I don't know," Zarah said. "They'll find a way around soon enough. I don't know. We just have to make it to the Flower. It's so close."

"It doesn't matter how close we are if they catch us," Alaric said. "Please, find us a way."

Zarah closed her eyes then took a deep breath. "No, no. That's too dangerous."

"It can't be more dangerous than Nikolos."

Zarah bit her lip. "It might be."

"Tell me!"

"There's a euphoria plant not far from here," Zarah said, "but it's dangerous. We could lose them, but you could lose yourself."

"I'll take that risk," Alaric said. "Let's go."

"I might lose you forever," Zarah said. "You might lose yourself forever."

"That's a danger you've faced all along," Alaric said.

"It's a danger I chose," Zarah said. "You shouldn't have to."

"Rook's dead," Alaric said. "The captain's dead. If I die, too, so be it. But you have to get to the World Flower and cure this plague. That's all that matters now."

Zarah nodded. "Follow me." She led Alaric onto a small, brightly flowered path.

"It's beautiful," Alaric said. "After the chaos and the danger, this is so peaceful." Even with the rage and violence storming up the main path, it still seemed peaceful. Alaric felt his heartbeat slowing and his mood lifting. The edges of his awareness grew soft and warm and comforted.

"Too peaceful," Zarah said.

"How can anything this beautiful be bad?" Alaric heard her words, but they seemed distant and indistinct. He wondered briefly if the World Flower was speaking through her again.

"Be careful," Zarah said. "We're almost there."

Just then, Nikolos and Damia charged in from the main path. In a moment, all four stopped. Around them, thick dark leaves formed a shaded room, lit by the glow of one hundred purple flowers.

"The treasure!" Alaric whispered.

"It's here!" Damia said, "I thought we lost it! I thought we lost our chance!"

Nikolos's arm lowered. The machete tumbled from his grasp. All the rage and tension left him. "I thought it was in the heart of the tree. It was here all along." He knelt and scooped up handfuls of gemstones. "Look! Jewels as big as grapes. Chains of finely wrought gold and platinum, untarnished by time." He lifted a thin circlet crown forged with intricate skill. The silvery metal shone in the light. A ruby the size of a small orange sparkled from the crown. "It's here. We have it. Sister, do you see it? Can you touch it too? We are as rich as kings."

"And queens." Damia sank to her knees, then lay down among the gems and jewelry. She found a crown of yellow gold set with emeralds as big as grapes. She laughed and placed it on her head. "Look at me. Queen Damia, the First."

Alaric knelt to touch the treasure. At first, he thought it might not be real. He refused to believe his eyes until he felt the cool, hard gems in his fingers. He let them run through his hand like grains of sand.

"The smallest of these could pay my way through the Academy. A second would set me up for life. Just one gem. Or two. I'll take two. I need two. If I took a third, I'd have a spare in case something happens to one of the others. If I took a fourth gem, I could pass wealth down to my children. But they're so small, I could fit five in my pocket. Five would fit easily. Maybe I'll take six." He stared down at the gems. "Zarah! Look at what I found! Zarah?"

The sound of her name felt heavy in Alaric's head. He thought he heard another name being called. It took him a moment to realize it was his own.

"Zarah, where are you?" Alaric looked around but could not see her. "You can go to the Flower. They won't chase you. We got what we came for. Zarah? Zarah?"

He heard that sound again, his name was being called from far away. He looked down at the gems. "This can't be a trick. These jewels are real, aren't they? I can feel them." Alaric squeezed his hands shut until the edges of the jewels pushed into his skin. "They are real." As the jewels pressed into his hand, he felt a chill in his body. "They're too real. They're realer than I am. And if I don't let them go, I'll stay here forever." He closed his eyes and threw the gems away. "Zarah!"

"Alaric!"

He reached out for her hand.

"Alaric, you can open your eyes now. I'm here."

Alaric opened his eyes. He saw the flowers across the wall, still glowing. He saw Nikolos and Damia rolling around the floor. They clutched seeds and sticks like precious gems. To their left lay the bones of some unfortunate man. He'd come there long ago and lost himself in his dreams. Perhaps those were the bones of Captain Valens himself.

Alaric shuddered. "Let's get out of here."

"Follow me," Zarah said. "The World Flower is nearby. We've almost reached the end of our journey."

Chapter 23

Zarah led Alaric up a steep path. The air smelled cool and wet among the dark leaves. Alaric felt a change in the atmosphere, an electric anticipation. Within a few moments, Zarah climbed out of the pathway to stand atop a broad platform.

Alaric followed. As he stuck his head up, he first saw the platform's edges, where deep green vines twined like a railing. Above, he saw the sky, blue with early evening, the first stars twinkling in the south. He stopped there, half in and out of the passage, staring up. "I never thought I'd see the sky again."

"Alaric, look," Zarah whispered.

The World Flower filled the eastern half of the platform. Its outer petals were a fair and peaceful blue, like the sky after a thunderstorm. Alaric could see nothing of its interior. The great flower slumped, folded up on itself. Even closed, the flower towered over them, at least eight feet tall.

"It looks dead," Alaric whispered. "Are we too late?"

Zarah reached out a trembling hand and touched the lowest petal. Light began to shine from within the flower. The blue grew translucent, and the bloom seemed to swell. The light quickly grew too intense for even the World Flower to contain. The great petals stretched and moved.

The World Flower opened a dozen feet across. It shimmered with every color Alaric knew and many he had never imagined.

Music grew from within the flower. Alaric felt it before he heard it. Later on, he would often say he was never sure that he'd heard it at all. But it was real, both unlike any other music and like all of them at once. The life and vigor of a hundred sea shanties rang out. He felt the lonesome drone of a mouth harp deep in his chest. The joyous trilling of a reed whistle moved him to dance. The delicate dance of harpist's fingers entranced him. The heartbreaking beauty of a fiddle in a master's hands moved him to tears.

Alaric dropped his gaze and bowed his head. "We are on holy ground." Yesterday he would have laughed at the idea of such a thing. But here, there was nothing else to say.

The brightness grew. It filled his vision but never quite blinded him.

Over the sound of the song, he heard Zarah speaking. "I'm here. I left my home and family. I crossed the sea, even the Shrouded Sea. I braved the thorns and lost some real friends. But I'm here. I'll do what you need. I'll do what you asked of me."

As Zarah spoke those words, the light wrapped around her like water.

All at once, a massive spray of golden pollen burst from the center of the World Flower. It shone and sparkled from within.

Alaric felt its healing power as it passed near him. He felt the bruises and scrapes of his battered body. He first felt them more intensely. So many he had forgotten, or not even noticed in his rush and terror. Then he felt them mending. The numb, grinding ache in his legs rose to sharp pain and then subsided.

All wounds must hurt to heal.

The pollen lifted into the sky and floated on a westward wind toward the Six Nations. The particles danced like a swarm of golden fireflies into the starlit sky. Alaric knew the plague was over and that the people of the Six Nations would be saved. He watched half the pollen float down to the island. Perhaps the World Flower would heal itself and break the curse of the thorn men.

"You did it, Zarah! You saved them! You saved us all." Alaric looked at Zarah. The glow wrapped around her. With each moment, it pulled her closer into the flower and its endless light. She was glowing herself. She was even turning translucent around the edges. "Zarah? What's happening?"

Zarah did not answer.

"Oh no. I'm not letting this happen." Alaric thought of how close he came to losing himself in the euphoria plant's embrace. "No. You rescued me. Now it's my turn." He grabbed her hand. "Zarah! Zarah!" He pulled, hoping that he could drag her away. But the plant kept hold, the light wrapping around her like endless arms.

A shining form emerged from the light at the heart of the World Flower. It stood Alaric's height and size, but it felt somehow much stronger, much more real.

"Let her go!" Alaric gave another hard pull on Zarah's hand, but his grip slipped. And then the luminous form was upon him. Its shining white hands clawed at his throat. Alaric threw his arms up and caught them by instinct alone.

They tumbled to the ground, wrestling. They rolled back and forth on the vine-walled platform. Alaric struggled to get to the top, to get free. He used every trick and move he knew, but the glowing form countered every one. Alaric struggled just to keep the shining one's hands from around his throat.

The brightness of his adversary filled Alaric's vision. Their struggles nearly drowned out the voiceless song. That moment somehow brought to mind one of his earliest memories. He stood alone on the docks, hungry, scared, begging for bread. He never knew his age, but he could not have been more than six years old. His belly was so empty it had stopped hurting and only felt a numb, aching hollowness.

An old man walked up. His skin was mottled, one eye milky and half-blind. Old Callan told him he'd have to work for his supper. He gave Alaric a job delivering messages all over Port Theron. In exchange, he got a corner to sleep in and two meals a day.

Alaric still hated Callan for using a half-starved child for cheap labor. For sending him up and down every dock and every berth, to every counting house and every warehouse in the city. Alaric remembered his short legs struggling to keep up. He remembered dodging out of the way of grown men who'd sooner run him down than give way.

A chill ran through Alaric. "Callan fed me and housed me and taught me every inch of Port Theron, and he never once hurt me." He almost lost his grip on the luminous stranger when he thought of how vulnerable he had been, how easily he could have ended up dead or broken. "That old wharf-rat saved my life."

Alaric focused on his adversary. "Enough!" He snarled and pushed forward, rolling the stranger onto his back. "Let her go!"

The glowing form said nothing but swung its hips around and brought Alaric onto his back again. Lennick sprung into Alaric's mind. A dock rat like Alaric had been, a cheap errand boy. Too young to be on his own. He thought about running from those two thugs. He remembered the rush of the chase, the exhilaration of escaping over the top of the fence. He'd helped Lennick get away and left those two goons empty-handed. He couldn't help but smile at that. He hoped the kid would learn his lesson and take safer jobs in the future.

"Are you doing this?" Alaric wrenched one hand free from the glowing man, then swung on top of him. Alaric scrambled to lock in a hold, to keep himself off the bottom, to keep the light-man's fingers off his neck. "Stop distracting me and let her go!"

The luminous stranger bucked like a wild horse. Alaric flew off his back and slammed into a wall of vines. The vine-railing gave but did not fall. Alaric almost lost consciousness with the force of the blow. In that half-conscious moment, Alaric saw his dream. He saw a classroom at the university in Hiberia. He saw himself taking classes with young men and women wearing scholars' robes. He saw himself graduating and taking his place as a professor. He saw himself walking through streets, the cap and robes of his station swirling around him. He felt the pride of what he had accomplished.

"Not what I have accomplished. What I might do." Alaric looked up at the glowing creature's featureless face. "I'm past that now. This is what matters. The cure. Zarah. Right here. Right now. Let her go!"

Without face or features, the luminous figure raged. Anger seethed out of it, a force Alaric could feel in his bones. It lunged forward, grappling with inhuman strength. Alaric slammed backward and rolled to the ground.

Another vision filled Alaric's head. At the university, in a lab, Professor Lamarca and a dozen students looked on. Alaric stood before a table full of bubbling, boiling beakers. He added two drops of some foul-smelling substance to another. Foam burst from the beaker and disgusting fumes filled the air. Glass shattered, and Lamarca rushed forward to pull it off the flame. The students gasped, then laughed. Lamarca pointed to the door.

Another vision, another room, a desk with endless stacks of books. Alaric read and read, but not to understand. Only to pass another test. The crowded stacks of books closed in on him. He dropped his head onto his hands, shaking in frustration, and wished he was back in Port Theron.

The vision shifted. Alaric saw himself crossing the stage, receiving a degree, earning the cap and gown of a scholar…and again found himself trapped in a small room with books that he could scarcely understand. This time, he only wanted to write something that would please a patron, a chancellor, or a publisher. A desperate fear gripped him. He felt all the hard-earned status slipping away. He saw years pass in the same crowded room. His hair grayed, his back bowed, his shoulders slumped, and his eyes grew weak and pale.

"Is that what you want?" Alaric asked. "Do you want me to admit it? Fine! I'll tell you what I've never told anyone. My biggest fear isn't failure. It's not being trapped on the docks all my life. My biggest fear is that I'll succeed but it won't change anything. That I'll do everything and feel just as trapped. That I'll get everything I ever wanted, and it will taste like seawater. Dirty, salty, sickening, undrinkable. And it will be too late to even spit it out."

Alaric opened his eyes and stared into the face of the glowing stranger. "This is me. I'm grappling with the divine, but I'm fighting against myself."

The luminous form did not answer, but the visions stopped.

"I can't fight you. You're me. I can't fear you. I can't hate you, not anymore. Because I can't hate and fear myself anymore. Whatever you're going to do to me, do it now." Alaric wrapped his arms around the glowing form.

Alaric. Alaric of no last name. The voice came from inside him, from the light, and from beyond even the World Flower. In the years to come, Alaric would never be sure if he had heard it all or only felt its truth. Alaric, you have been fearful and greedy. You have been selfish and deceptive. But you have never been alone, never been unloved. I know you, and I love you. I, who gave the seasons their orderly march. I, who gave the storms their unpredictable chaos. I, who gave the tiger her claws and the deer his swift feet. You are my child, and I have always loved you. You did not earn that, no more than you earned Old Callan's help, no more than Lennick earned yours. And you can never lose it.

Alaric leaned into the embrace, feeling truly at peace for the first time he could remember. He stayed still, wrapped in the light, for as long as it lasted.

Zarah stepped free of the petals. The World Flower stood open, healthy and bright. Shining gold pollen still sparkled down around them and floated down to the island below. "Alaric, we did it."

"Zarah!" Alaric rushed to her and grabbed her in a hug. After a moment, he let go and stepped back awkwardly. "Sorry."

"Don't apologize. I'm glad to see you too," Zarah whispered. "I might not have come back if you hadn't gone in. It would have been so easy to walk into the glory and be gone forever." She shivered. "I'm glad you saved me, but I'll always miss that feeling."

"Me too."

Bright green vines rose up toward the platform. Each tangled nest held a person. The scholars were the first to rise. Maxime and Lamarca blinked themselves back into consciousness.

Next came Rook Corbin. His left hand rubbed his shoulder beneath his cut shirt. "I don't believe it. I felt that blade go in. I thought I was a dead man."

The captain was the last to rise. In all the chaos and the fall from the platform, she'd still managed to keep her hat. "Well, that was unexpected. Rook! You're alive!"

"Yeah! I can hardly believe it myself!" Rook looked around for a moment and frowned. "Hey, are you sure we're not all dead? I mean, I was hoping for a few more people, but I could imagine worse afterlifes. Afterlives?"

Alaric laughed in spite of himself. "From what Zarah and I have seen, the afterlife is better than this." He and Zarah shared a glance, longing for a world they would not again reach in this lifetime.

"Then I declare that I am no longer afraid of dying." Maxime stared up at the World Flower. "It's beautiful. Does anyone else hear the singing? Or…it's more like a symphony, but not only the instruments that would ordinarily be in a symphony. All kinds of instruments, from every nation, both elevated and common. It's…it's…."

"This place is a miracle, if Maxime is at a loss for words." Lamarca stared at the World Flower for a few minutes, and they all joined her in silence. She took a deep breath and smiled gently. "It is good to see you all. And to see that. I have to admit, I never for a minute believed we would see the World Flower. I thought Zarah might, if we did everything right, but I had no hope of making it this far."

Jill held out her hand and caught a grain of pollen. It danced upon her palm, twinkling like a golden star. Then, it caught some mystic wind and blew away to the west. "So, is this what healed us?"

"Yes." Zarah closed her eyes and breathed deeply, communing once more with the Flower. "Most of the pollen is blowing away on the west wind. It's already flowing north to Solok, southwest to Thervingi, south to Katargo, and further on to Hiberia. The cure will reach our homeland by morning."

"We don't even have to go back and deliver the cure?" Jill asked.

Zarah took a deep breath. "The island wants to know what to do about Nikolos and Damia. They're healed and happy, but they're trapped by the euphoria flower. The island can't feed them. They won't hurt, but they will die."

Alaric looked at Rook and at the captain, then at Zarah. "I'm not the one they hurt. I'm not the one who should decide. But I was trapped in the euphoria flower. I don't think Nikolos and Damia would want to die that way. I know I wouldn't."

"Captain." Rook rubbed his shoulder, then rotated it. He smiled in spite of himself. "My shoulder hasn't felt this good in fifteen years. I've got no grudge, really, but I don't want this to happen again. It's you he betrayed, and it's you who will have to watch him close. If he does return."

Jill frowned. "Miss Remei?"

"If you promise to watch them, I will consent," Zarah said. "I don't trust them, but I won't call for their deaths either. Not even a peaceful, painless death." She grew very stern and fixed the captain with the gaze that caused even the great Jill Crimson to flinch. "But it's got to be both of them, not just your brother. If you're going to show mercy, it can't just be to your family."

"I understand," Jill said, "and you're right. I can't free one and leave the other. And if I did rescue only one, it would have to be the lower ranked one. My brother was the first mate and bore the greater responsibility." She frowned. "Two will be harder to control than one, but I'm up to the task. You can tell the Flower to let them go." She paused. "Ask the Flower to let them go. I'm far past trying to impose my will on this place."

A few minutes later, Nikolos and Damia walked up the path. Their eyes seemed far away and dreamy, like they hadn't completely awakened. Damia reached out with both hands, touching little bits of pollen. The little twinkling gold sparks circled around her hands for a moment then blew away on the wind. She and Nikolos were as healed and whole as the others.

Alaric hoped for the best, but he mostly felt distrust. Then Nikolos saw his sister. The big man's face lit up with shock, disbelief, and utter joy. It was quickly shadowed by guilt. That told Alaric all he needed to know.

"You made the right decision, Captain," Alaric said.

The captain moved to embrace her brother. "I know."

Epilogue

Alaric stood upon the deck of the Scarlet Gray, looking back on the Isle of the World Flower. The descent from the top of the great tower had been peaceful and easy, but no less wondrous than the trip up. There were so many things of beauty and wonder Alaric had missed when he was fighting for his life. So many colors of flowers. So many fruiting branches and variegated leaves. All twisting on vines suspended delicately, as if gravity could not touch them.

The golden pollen and the rejuvenation of the World Flower had driven all trace of the thorn men away. Even the great rotted heart had burned away. In its place was a bright green tangle of fresh new growth.

"I wonder if the treasure really was in there," Rook had said.

The captain laughed. "We'll not find out now."

"What if it was?" The idea had occurred to Alaric at that very moment, though he wondered why he hadn't thought of it before. "The thorn men had to come from somewhere. What could corrupt a sacred place like a treasure that was twice blood money? First the pirates stole it from their victims. Then Valens stole it from his own men."

"Well, it appears to be healed now," Professor Lamarca said. "Thanks to Zarah—and to you."

The seaweed let them pass easily. The crew had been only slightly disappointed that no treasure had been found. Most of them had their doubts from the beginning. They were more worried about seeing their captain and crewmates again. In the end, curing the plague was enough reason to celebrate. The captain opened three barrels of the best.

Captain Jill Crimson stepped to the railing beside Alaric, a cup of hot coffee in each hand. She offered one to Alaric.

"Coffee? On board the ship?" Alaric asked. "You are celebrating."

"You've earned it," the captain said. "From dock rat to Hero of the Isle of the World Flower. Perhaps I should call you Alaric Thorn-Slayer."

"Please don't," he said with a chuckle. "Just Alaric is fine."

"Very well, Alaric," Jill said. "Where do we go from here?"

"I thought you were the captain of the ship."

"I am." Jill grinned. "And don't you forget it. But I thought my passengers might have a say. You and Zarah are the reason we're still among the living. I won't soon forget that." She gestured to the ocean and the wall the fog beyond. "She still hears the World Flower, but it's not painful or confusing anymore. She said it will guide her, guide us, if we want it to. She said she can find the rest of the islands. We can sail the Shrouded Sea with all its wonders and terrors. We can find marvels and miracles no one has ever seen before."

"What does Zarah think of that plan?" Alaric asked.

"Zarah and the scholars think it's a fine idea," Jill said. "My crew is relatively enthusiastic. The skeptics can be convinced. But you get a say. After all you've done, you have the right to say, 'take me home.' You've earned the right to take your portion of the pay—and the treasure we didn't find—and go back to Port Theron."

Alaric raised his cup. "First, a drink to Zarah Remei."

"And a drink to Alaric. Just Alaric." The captain clinked her cup to his, and they drank. The coffee was hot and strong. It wasn't as smooth or rich as what the coffeehouse had served them, but that didn't matter to Alaric. "Now, answer my question. Do you want to take your money and go home? You've earned that right."

Alaric's smile broke across his face, as wide and as bright as a sunrise. "Why would I ever want to do that? There's a brand-new world to find, and people who need me right here."

Author's Note

Hello! Thanks for reading *The Shrouded Sea*. I hope you loved Alaric and Zarah's story (I really loved writing it).

If you did, and you'd like more information about upcoming stories and novels, head over to leondedeaux.com and join my mailing list. You'll always get a free (e-book) story for signing up, and you'll get more info on my projects, process, and such. I'd love to hear from you there.

I'd also really appreciate it if you left a review on Amazon. Every review helps. I love the feedback, and reviews help readers decide if my books are right for them. You can find my Amazon page at https://www.amazon.com/Leon-Dedeaux/e/B004SSIPL6

Keep reading for a special preview of *The Manticore and the Woodcutter's Daughter*, the first book in the Divine Stones Series, coming soon.

Thanks again!

Leon

The Manticore and the Woodcutter's Daughter

Footsteps pounded on the old logging road. Polly stood, stepping clear of the sheep and into the path. She squared her shoulders, ready for whatever news may come.

"Polly, Merry, Mrs. Barrow!" Peter, the youngest man on Father's team, rushed out of the woods, his face as pale as a dead man's. Mother's face grew just as pale. The woods were a dangerous place and logging dangerous work. They had been fearing news like this for a long time. "It - your -" the young man panted, stumbling over his words.

"Calm down." Polly caught Peter by the shoulders and held him steady. "What happened? Did a tree fall on him? Did he fall? Was it the wolf?"

"This, this was no mortal beast." Peter took a deep breath and forced himself to stop shaking. "Not wolf, nor bear, nor cat."

"What was it then?" Polly said.

"Red fur, like a bloodhound. Wings stretching twice the height of a man. It towered over your father like a bear. Claws like a cat. A tail like a serpent's sting. And its face was neither man nor beast." With each word Peter grew paler, and Polly feared he might faint if he continued. "It flew down and stung him then it leapt into the air and flew away without a sound. It didn't even look at us."

"Where is he?"

"The men are bringing him," Peter whispered, "he's alive, but barely. He sleeps a sleep as deep as death. We'd have thought him dead if not for the rise and fall of his chest."

Polly dropped Peter and raced down the path, rushing into the woods to meet her father's men. They'd tied together a litter from fresh-cut branches and carried her father between them, two men on front and two on back.

"Daddy!" She raced to her father and gathered him up in her arms.

"Polly -" Jacob, the team foreman said, "let us carry him. He's the biggest man among us. You'll never get him home by yourself, girl."

Polly lifted her father from his litter. "Bring in the day's lumber. I'll carry him."

"Carry him if you will," Jacob said, "but we'll not leave you 'til we see you both home."

Polly laid her father out upon her own bed, a pallet of hay covered with patchwork quilts. "Rest, we will see you through this sickness."

The men behind her muttered among themselves. "Polly, girl -"

Polly turned, her green eyes wide and hard as the sea. "Don't you dare declare him dead. His chest rises and falls. He breathes in and out. His heart beats, and his face is warm to the touch. He is sick, wounded, but not dead. Remember that, or you'll answer to me."

Mama's cool touch took her by surprise. "Come, daughter, walk with me."

"Yes, Mama."

"Woodcutting is a dangerous way of life," her mother said, "do you think I had not prepared for this? Do you think I had not rehearsed this in my mind ten hundred times? Do you think I haven't dreaded this day all my life?"

Polly turned, surprised by the steel in her mother's voice.

"Did you think me a fool? True, I have more of Merry's girlishness than your somber solidness, but surely -"

"No, Mama, of course not," Polly said, "but I never thought of you thinking of... this."

Her Mama smiled. "Ah, to be young again. The world revolved around me when I was young, too. If anyone tells you different, they're either lying or forgetful." She motioned to Merry. "I need your help to shear the sheep, pretty one."

"You want her to help you shear the sheep?" Polly said, "It's a good thing Grumpus is done."

"She can occupy her mind with work, or with grieving. I'll not give the poor girl the choice."

"Ah, then what do you want me to do?" Polly said, "Succumb to despair?"

"Don't be sarcastic. It doesn't suit you," Mama said, "You are already planning to search for a cure."

Polly couldn't help but smile. "You know me well, Mama. Where do I start?"

"This creature, it seems so familiar," Mama said, "like it's lurking at the edge of my memory, just out of sight, waiting to strike."

Polly's eyes widened. "You've seen it before?"

"No, no," Mama said, "I would not have forgotten it, though I were an unweaned child. But perhaps I heard the story, long ago? I don't know what she knows, but there is an old woman in the village. She may be the oldest person within a hundred leagues, and her mind is still sharp as a maiden's. Go to her. If anyone here knows the cure for a flying beast's sting, she will."

"And the doctor?"

"I sent Peter for him as soon as you ran down the path," Mama said, "but we both know he can't cure this. Go, strong one, save the man I love."

The old woman's house sat on the very edge of the village. It was little more than a hut, small, old-fashioned, and slowly decaying. Strong smells assaulted Polly before she even reached the doorway, herbs and tinctures and essences, pungent, sweet, musky, and spicy all at once.

"Great Auntie, may I enter?" Polly said loudly. She couldn't knock: a time-worn deer skin served as the only door. She shivered just a little: the deer skin could scarcely keep the wind out in the springtime, much less the winter's cold blast. How could this woman's children and grandchildren leave her in such disarray?

"Come in, dearie," a frail voice answered from inside.

Polly pushed the deerskin aside and stepped inside, ducking her head to get through the doorway. The hut was dark, lit only by a small peat fire. As Polly's eyes adjusted, she saw the woman, wrapped in a wolf's pelt, clutching a thin candle.

Great Auntie might have been a hundred years old, or more. Time had shrunk her inward, wrinkling her skin, bowing her back, and drawing her hands into claws. Maybe her children and grandchildren had not abandoned her. Maybe she'd outlived them all.

"Elder," Polly said, bowing her head in respect, "I need your wisdom, your knowledge."

The woman laughed weakly. "I have not heard those words in a very long time, dearie." She drew the breath for each word like water from a deep well, slowly and with great effort.

"Will you help me?"

"Yes, of course, dearie. Perhaps I have been kept alive for just such a day as this." Her eyes twinkled, and Polly realized her mother was right. No matter how much time had ravaged her body, it had not touched the woman's mind.

"My father and his crew were cutting wood in the forest, and a beast flew in. It landed beside my father, stung him, and flew away before any of his friends could react. It took no notice of them, gave no warning, and left as quickly as it had come."

The air was thick with peat-smoke, and Polly's eyes watered at the sweet, choking burn. Or that's what she told herself. No tears for her father. That was her rule. He was still alive, and she would save him. No tears.

"What did this beast look like?" Great Auntie leaned forward just a bit, pressing her arthritic hands together.

"I wasn't there," Polly said, "they said it had red fur, wings twice a man's height across, claws like a cat's, and a tail like a serpent's sting. It was bigger than father, perhaps as big as a bear."

"Manticore," the old woman said.

"Man-tick-what?"

"Manticore. The herald of the great Ancient One." Great Auntie raised two fingers to her eyes and jerked them away in superstitious disgust. "May it never rise again."

"Manticore?" Polly said, "Ancient One? I don't care about the Ancient One."

"You should. You know nothing of its time. Even my grandmother's grandmother did not. But the tales were passed down, tales of blood and fire and pain." Her frail form shuddered in the darkness. "Born of mortal pain and heat, awakened by the dark star's fall. Blood and fire and pain."

"I just want to cure my father," Polly whispered.

"There is no cure in our village, but nearby, perhaps." She turned her deep, sparkling black eyes on Polly. "Are you brave, young one? Are you truly brave?"

Polly met her gaze. "Tell me what to do."

The old woman cackled, a sharp, high, explosive sound like an eruption of terrified hens. "I have told you all I know. You must seek one even older than I, one who remembers the Dark Age."

"Older than you?" Polly said.

"Older, perhaps, than my grandmother," Great Auntie said, "He will know."

"Where do I start?"

"You must walk the Manticore's Pathway, young one. The path leads through the dark valley and up the Raven's Hill. A short flight for a winged creature, but a cruel, difficult journey for earthbound mortals," Great Auntie said, "You must go there alone. He will not see you otherwise. The hermit will know what to do."

"Will he know the cure?"

"He will know what to do, dearie," Great Auntie said, "of that I am certain."

"Are you sure he still lives, Elder?" Polly wondered when Great Auntie had last seen the hermit. Had it been ten years? Fifty?

Great Auntie laughed. "He lives. If ever he died, we would all know it. Now go!"